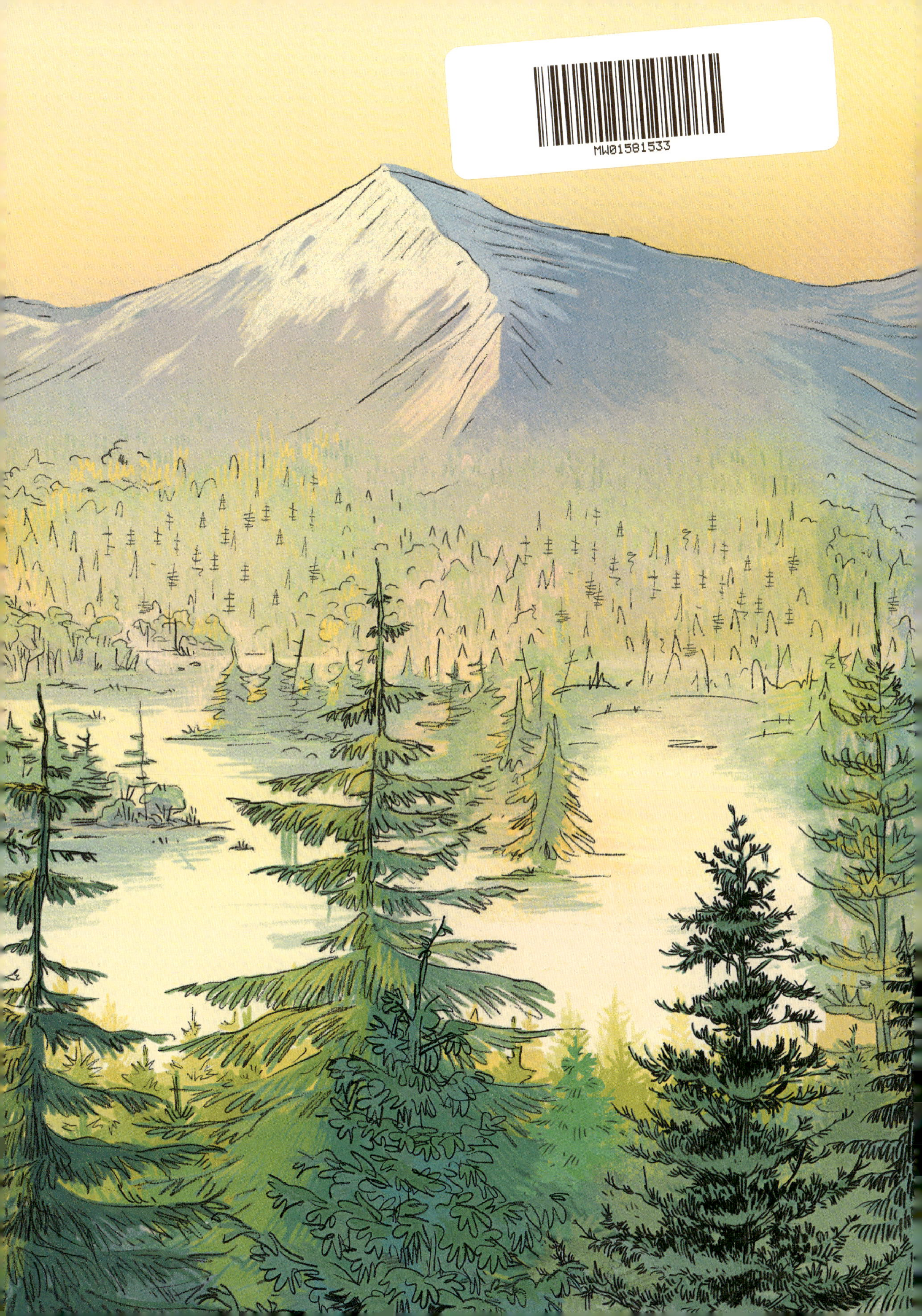

Who's who?

Gigi

Age: 12

Interests: Tiny creatures, big adventures

Wilderness skills: Calm in hairy situations. Chief navigator – can find her way with a map, the stars and a little intuition.

Moyo

Age: 14

Interests: Doodling (constantly)

Wilderness skills: A forager's eye. Moyo learned everything he knows about foraging wild foods at forest school, where he crammed his notebook with useful lists and drawings.

Uncle Dee

Age: 42

Interests: Building boats

Wilderness skills: Loads. Dee spends his life out in nature, and has been kayaking, trekking and mountaineering in some of the world's wildest places.

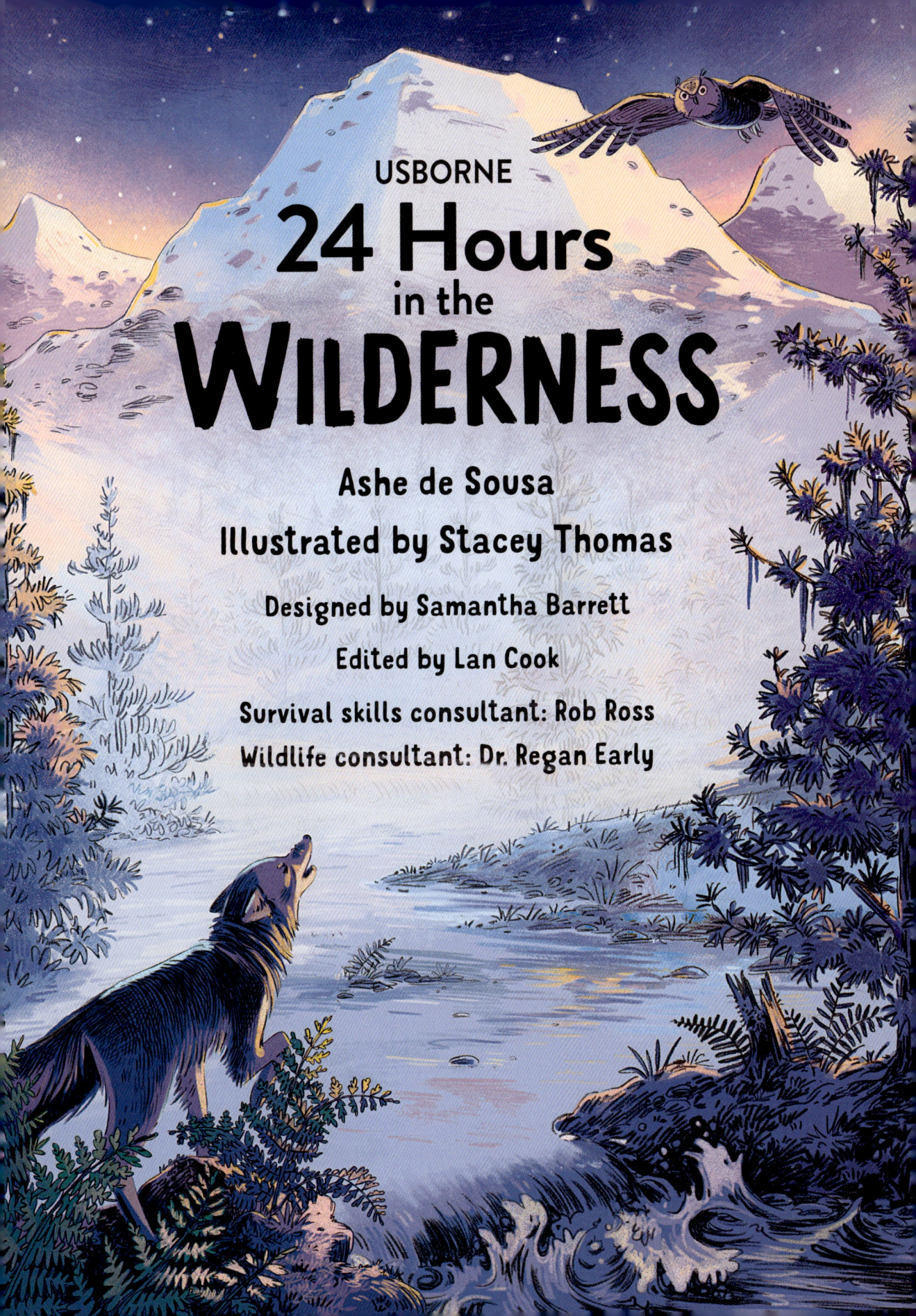

Usborne
24 Hours in the WILDERNESS

Ashe de Sousa

Illustrated by Stacey Thomas

Designed by Samantha Barrett

Edited by Lan Cook

Survival skills consultant: Rob Ross
Wildlife consultant: Dr. Regan Early

Usborne Quicklinks

For links to websites and videos where you can trek deep into some of the world's wildest places, spot wildlife and hone your wilderness survival skills, go to usborne.com/Quicklinks and type in the title of this book.

Here are some of the things you can do at the websites we recommend:

- Listen to the haunting song of a coastal wolf
- Watch hungry grizzly bears catch spawning salmon in mid-air
- Master dozens of knots with simple animated guides
- Test your knowledge of poisonous plants with a quiz
- See survival skills in action, from fire starting to foraging

Usborne Publishing is not responsible for the content of external websites. Children should be supervised online. Please follow the online safety guidelines at usborne.com/Quicklinks

This story takes place in the Great Bear Rainforest, a large area of protected wilderness in the Pacific Northwest, Canada. This is the territory of 26 First Nations groups, people whose ancestors have lived here for thousands of years. They have long acted as stewards, protecting the land and the creatures that live here.

CONTENTS

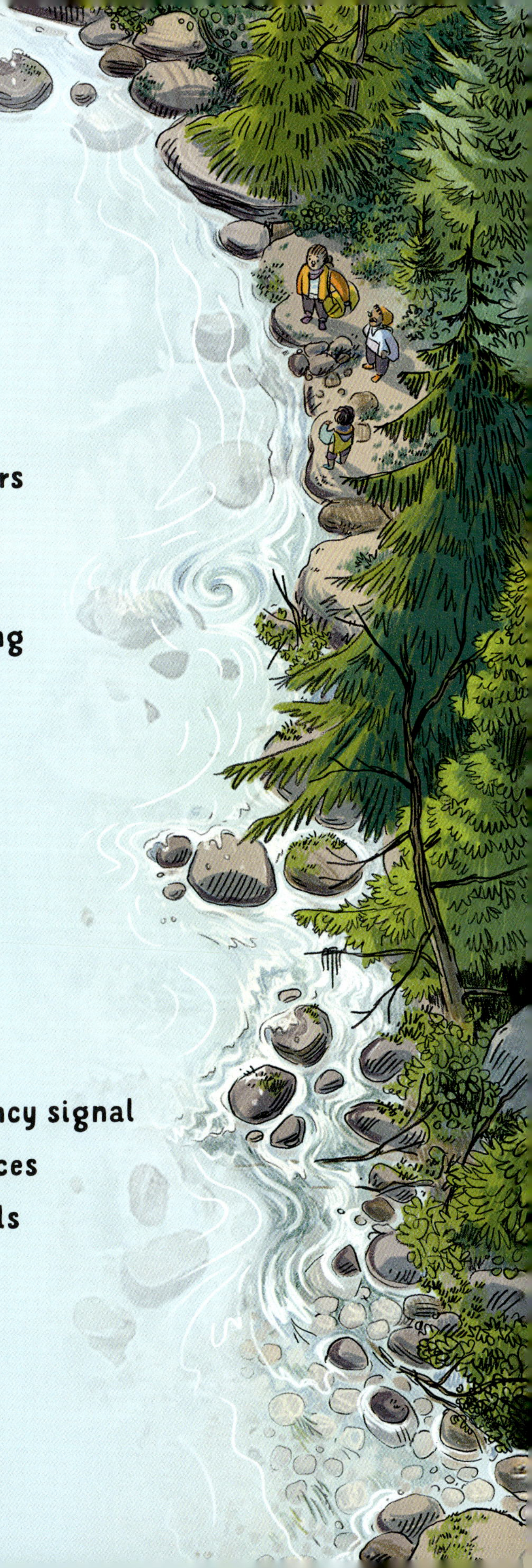

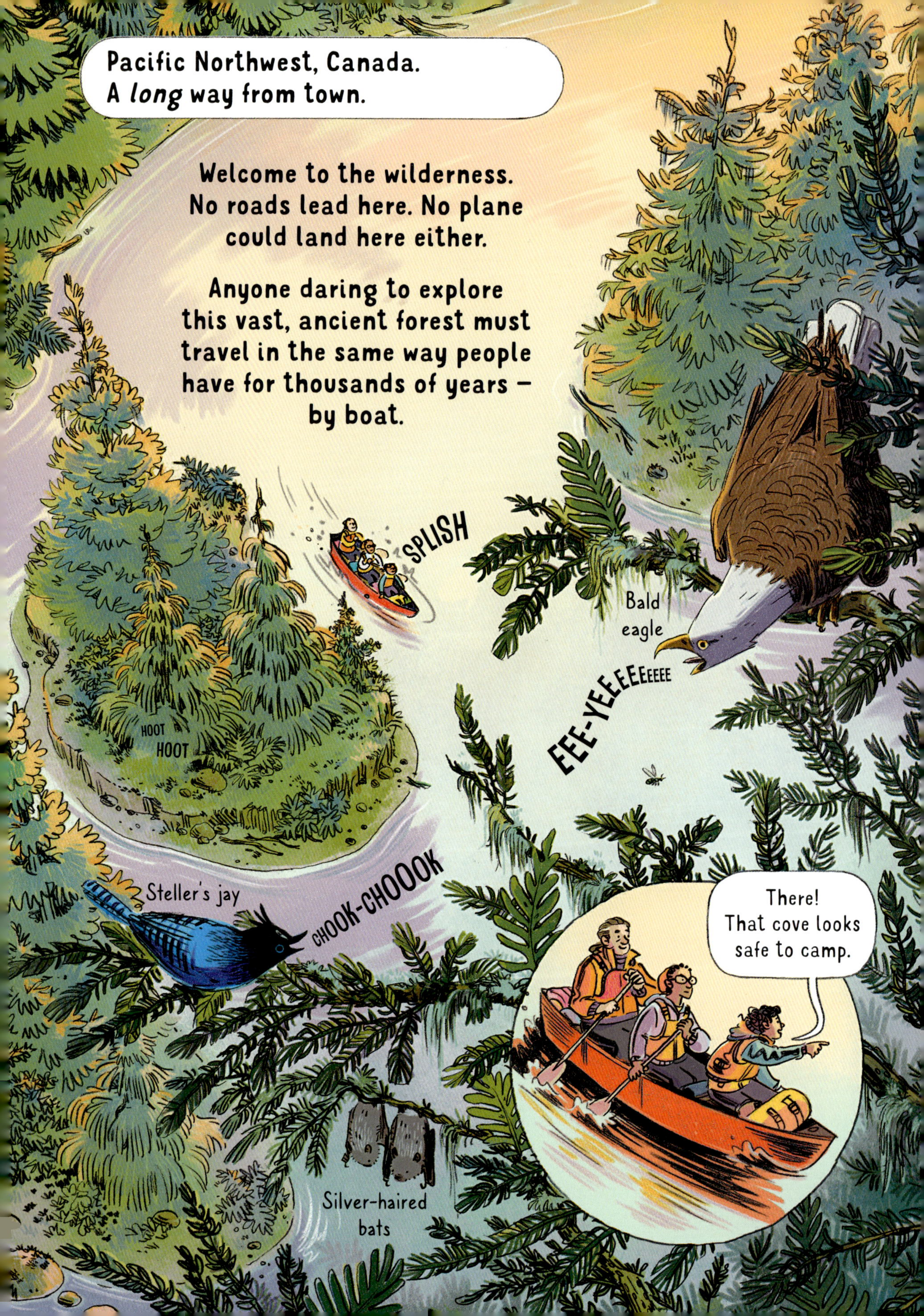
Pacific Northwest, Canada.
A *long* way from town.
Welcome to the wilderness. No roads lead here. No plane could land here either.
Anyone daring to explore this vast, ancient forest must travel in the same way people have for thousands of years – by boat.
SPLISH
Bald eagle
EEE-YEEEEEeeee
HOOT
HOOT
Steller's jay
CHOOK-CHOOOK
There! That cove looks safe to camp.
Silver-haired bats

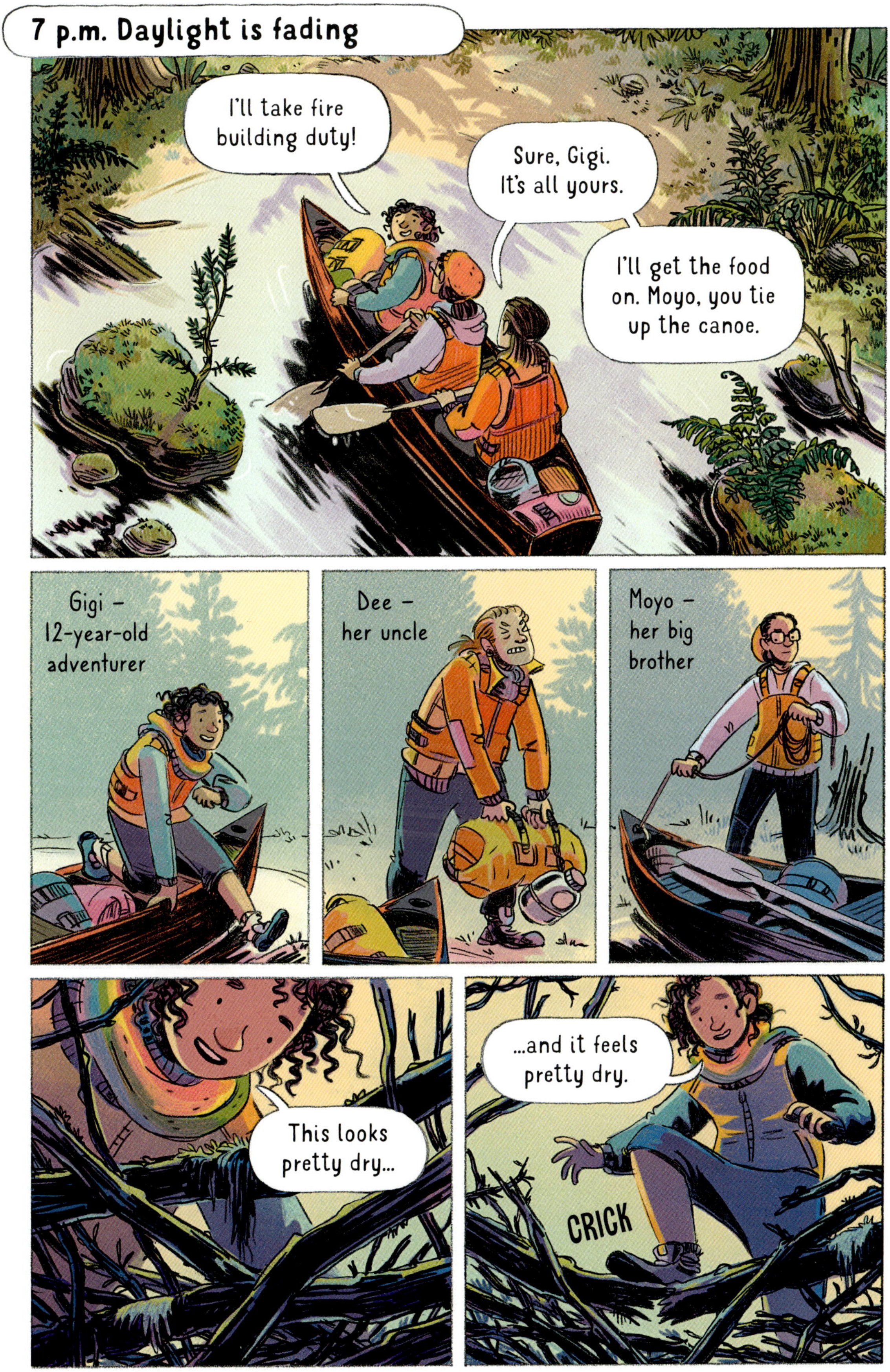
7 p.m. Daylight is fading
I'll take fire building duty!
Sure, Gigi. It's all yours.
I'll get the food on. Moyo, you tie up the canoe.
Gigi – 12-year-old adventurer
Dee – her uncle
Moyo – her big brother
This looks pretty dry...
...and it feels pretty dry.
CRICK

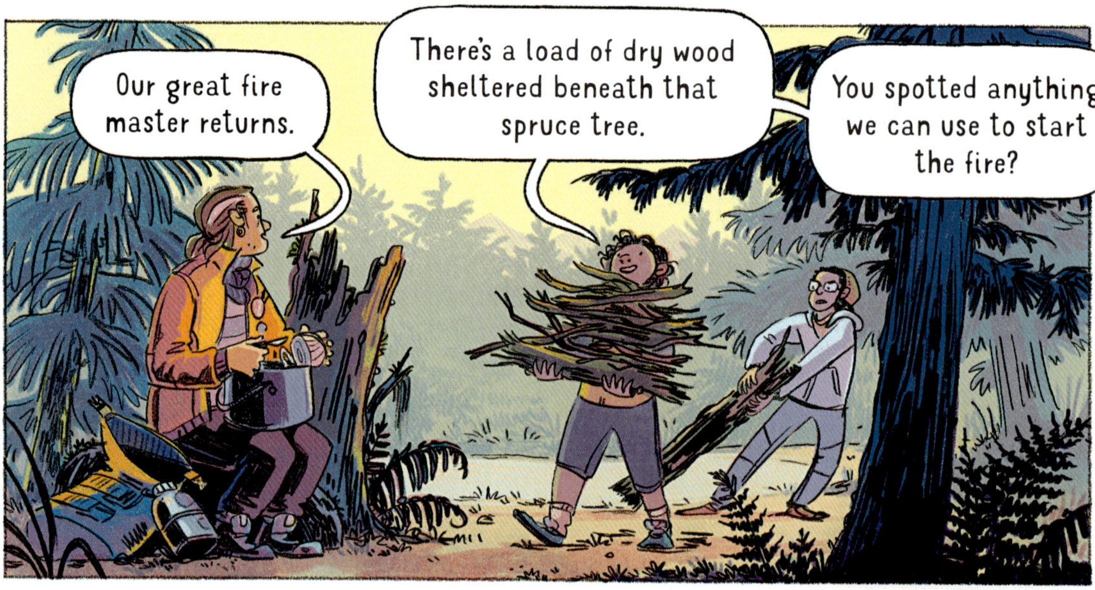
Our great fire master returns.
There's a load of dry wood sheltered beneath that spruce tree.
You spotted anything we can use to start the fire?

Finding natural fire starter

To get a fire going, you need *tinder* – that's light, dry stuff that burns easily.

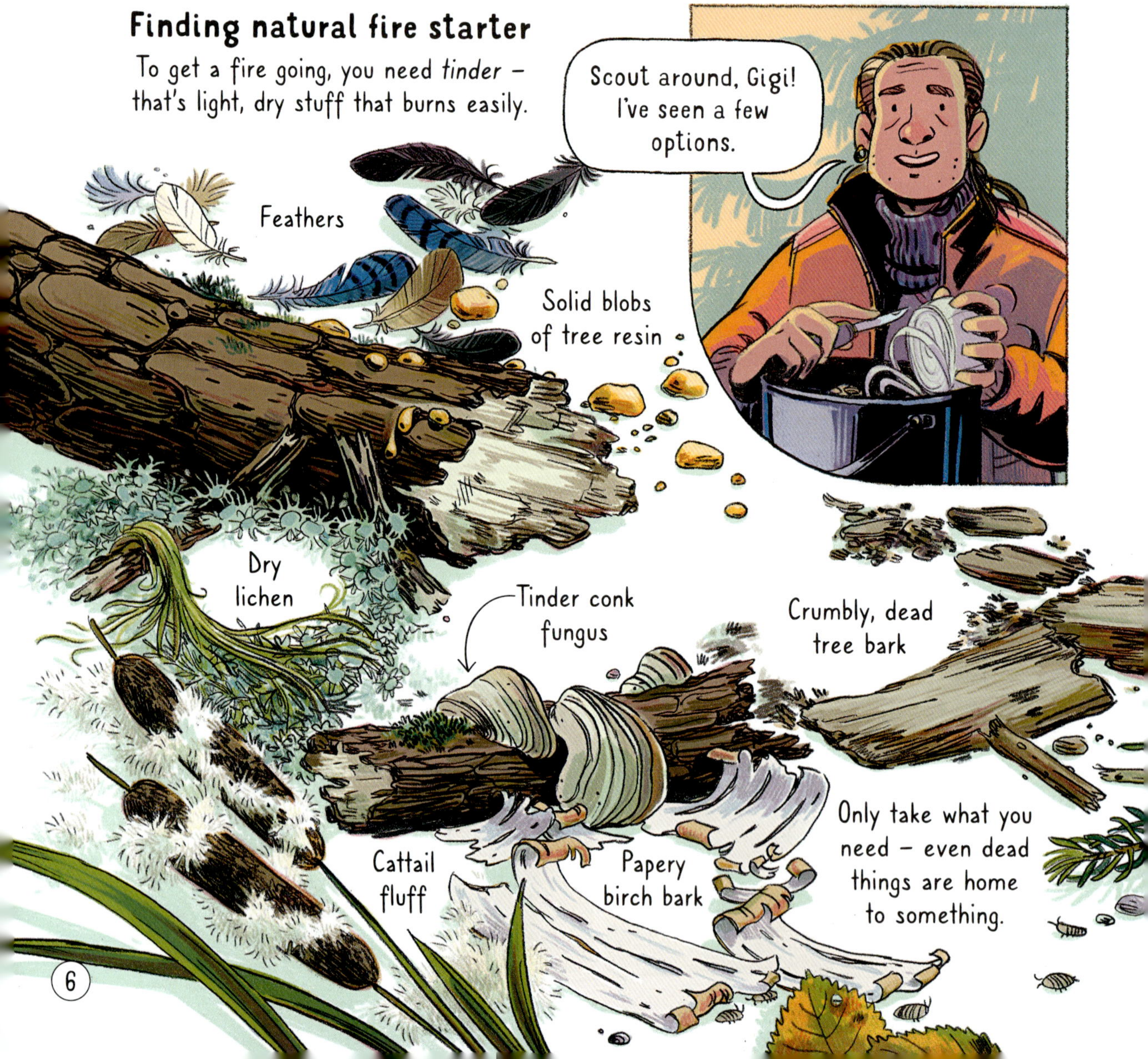
Scout around, Gigi! I've seen a few options.
Feathers
Solid blobs of tree resin
Dry lichen
Tinder conk fungus
Crumbly, dead tree bark
Cattail fluff
Papery birch bark
Only take what you need – even dead things are home to something.

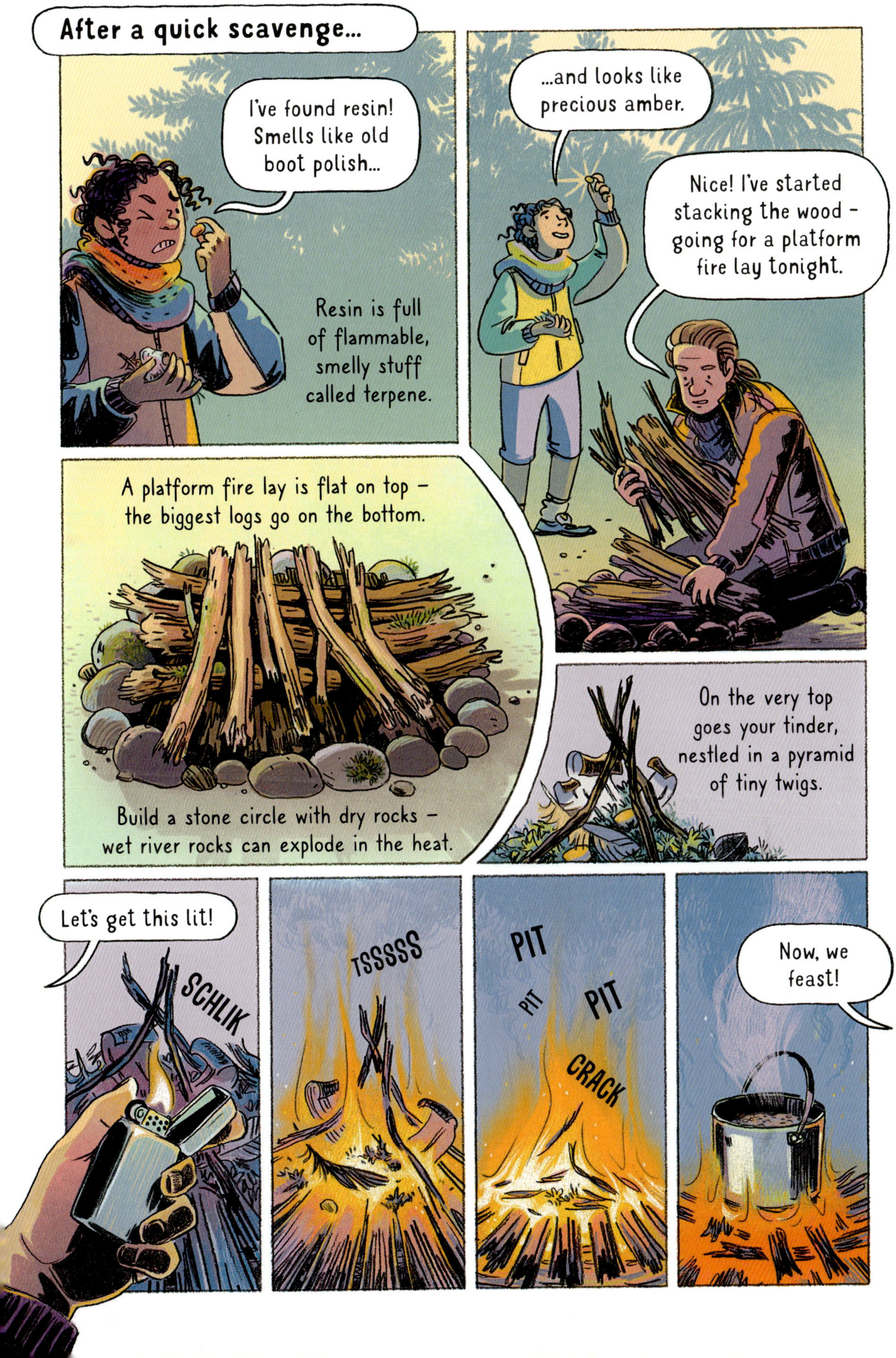
After a quick scavenge...
I've found resin! Smells like old boot polish...
Resin is full of flammable, smelly stuff called terpene.
...and looks like precious amber.
Nice! I've started stacking the wood – going for a platform fire lay tonight.
A platform fire lay is flat on top – the biggest logs go on the bottom.
Build a stone circle with dry rocks – wet river rocks can explode in the heat.
On the very top goes your tinder, nestled in a pyramid of tiny twigs.
Let's get this lit!
SCHLIK
TSSSSS
PIT
PIT
PIT
CRACK
Now, we feast!

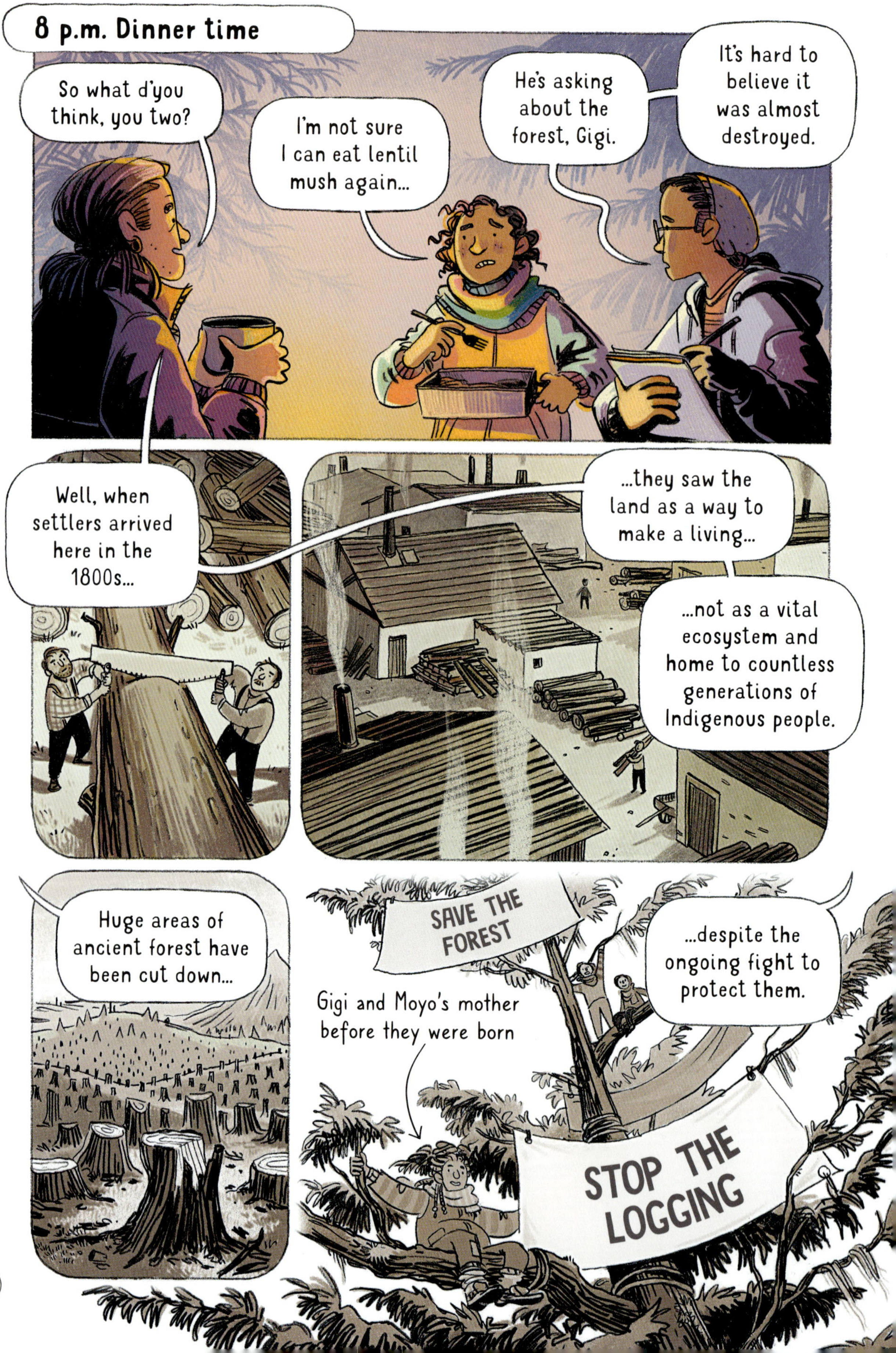
8 p.m. Dinner time
So what d'you think, you two?
I'm not sure I can eat lentil mush again...
He's asking about the forest, Gigi.
It's hard to believe it was almost destroyed.
Well, when settlers arrived here in the 1800s...
...they saw the land as a way to make a living...
...not as a vital ecosystem and home to countless generations of Indigenous people.
Huge areas of ancient forest have been cut down...
SAVE THE FOREST
Gigi and Moyo's mother before they were born
...despite the ongoing fight to protect them.
STOP THE LOGGING

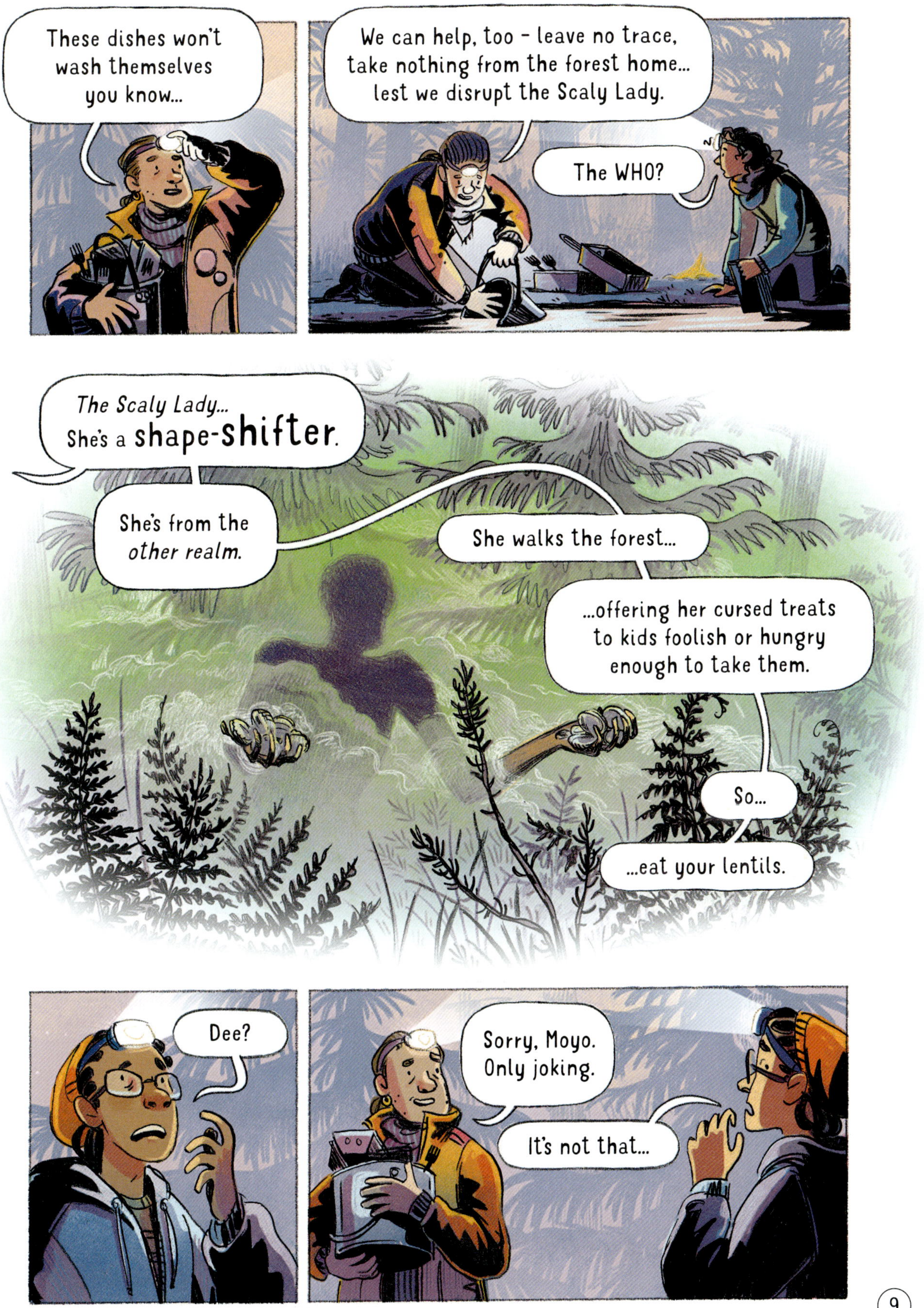

These dishes won't wash themselves you know...
We can help, too - leave no trace, take nothing from the forest home... lest we disrupt the Scaly Lady.
The WHO?
The Scaly Lady... She's a shape-shifter.
She's from the other realm.
She walks the forest...
...offering her cursed treats to kids foolish or hungry enough to take them.
So...
...eat your lentils.
Dee?
Sorry, Moyo. Only joking.
It's not that...

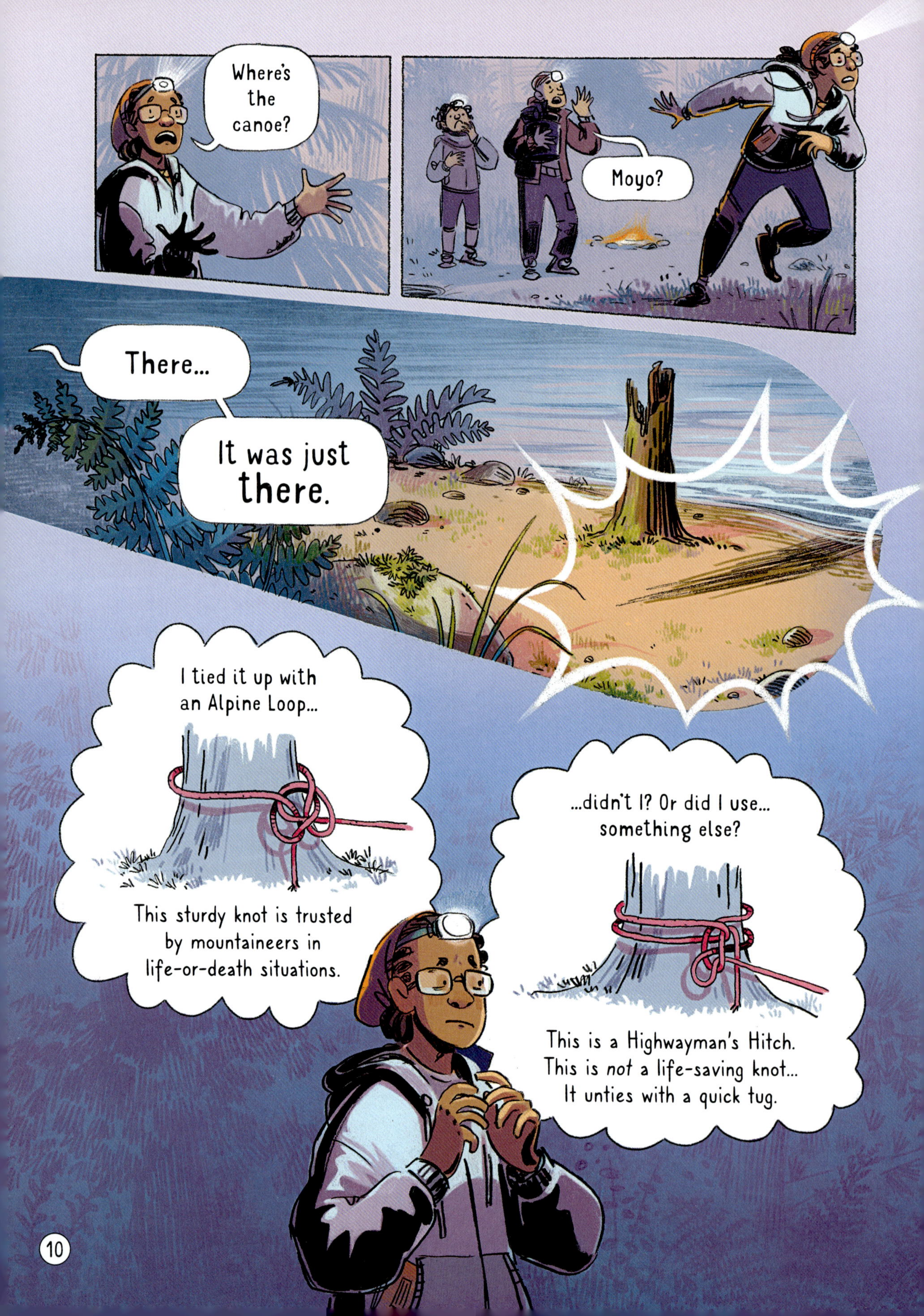
Where's the canoe?
Moyo?
There...
It was just there.
I tied it up with an Alpine Loop...
This sturdy knot is trusted by mountaineers in life-or-death situations.
...didn't I? Or did I use... something else?
This is a Highwayman's Hitch. This is *not* a life-saving knot... It unties with a quick tug.

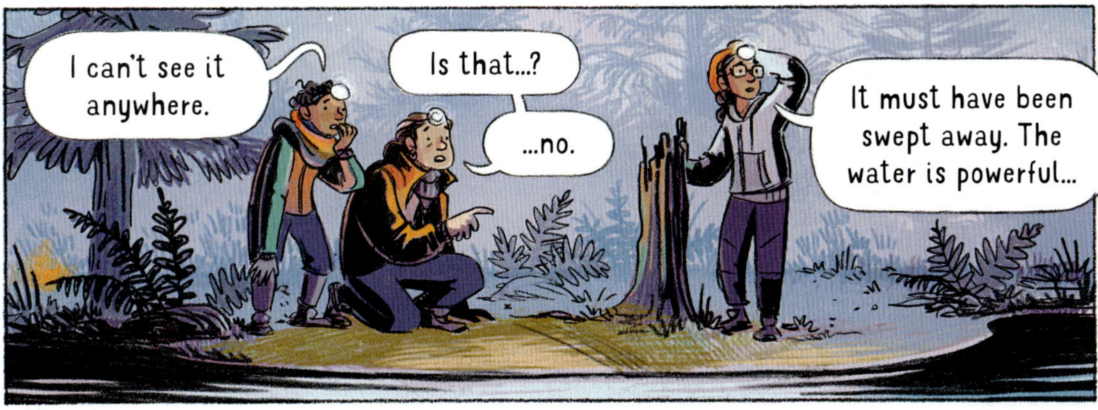
I can't see it anywhere.
Is that...?
...no.
It must have been swept away. The water is powerful...

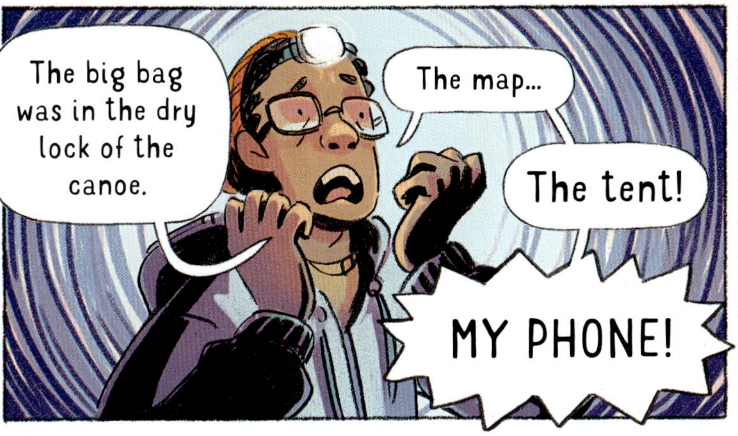
The big bag was in the dry lock of the canoe.
The map...
The tent!
MY PHONE!

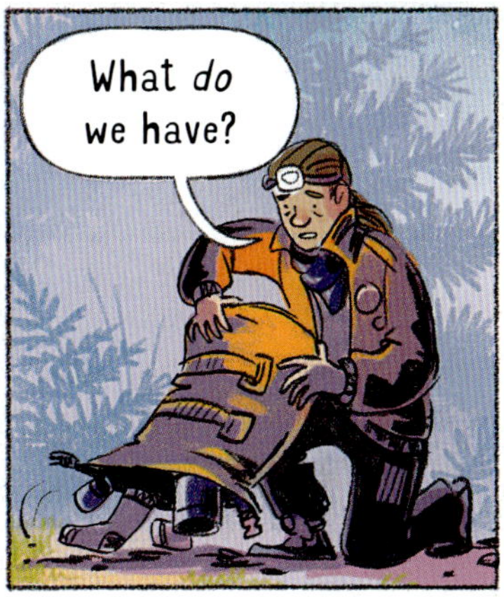
What *do* we have?

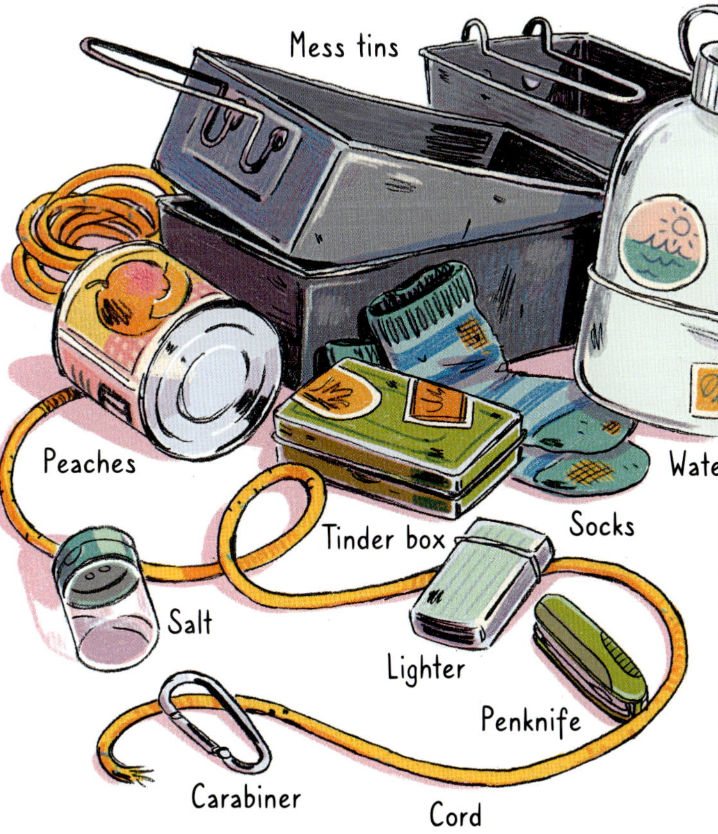
Mess tins
Pan
Peaches
Water bottle
Tinder box
Socks
Salt
Lighter
Penknife
Carabiner
Cord

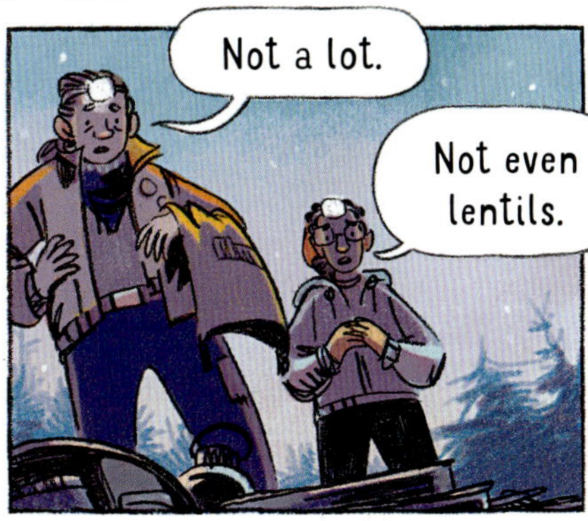
Not a lot.
Not even lentils.

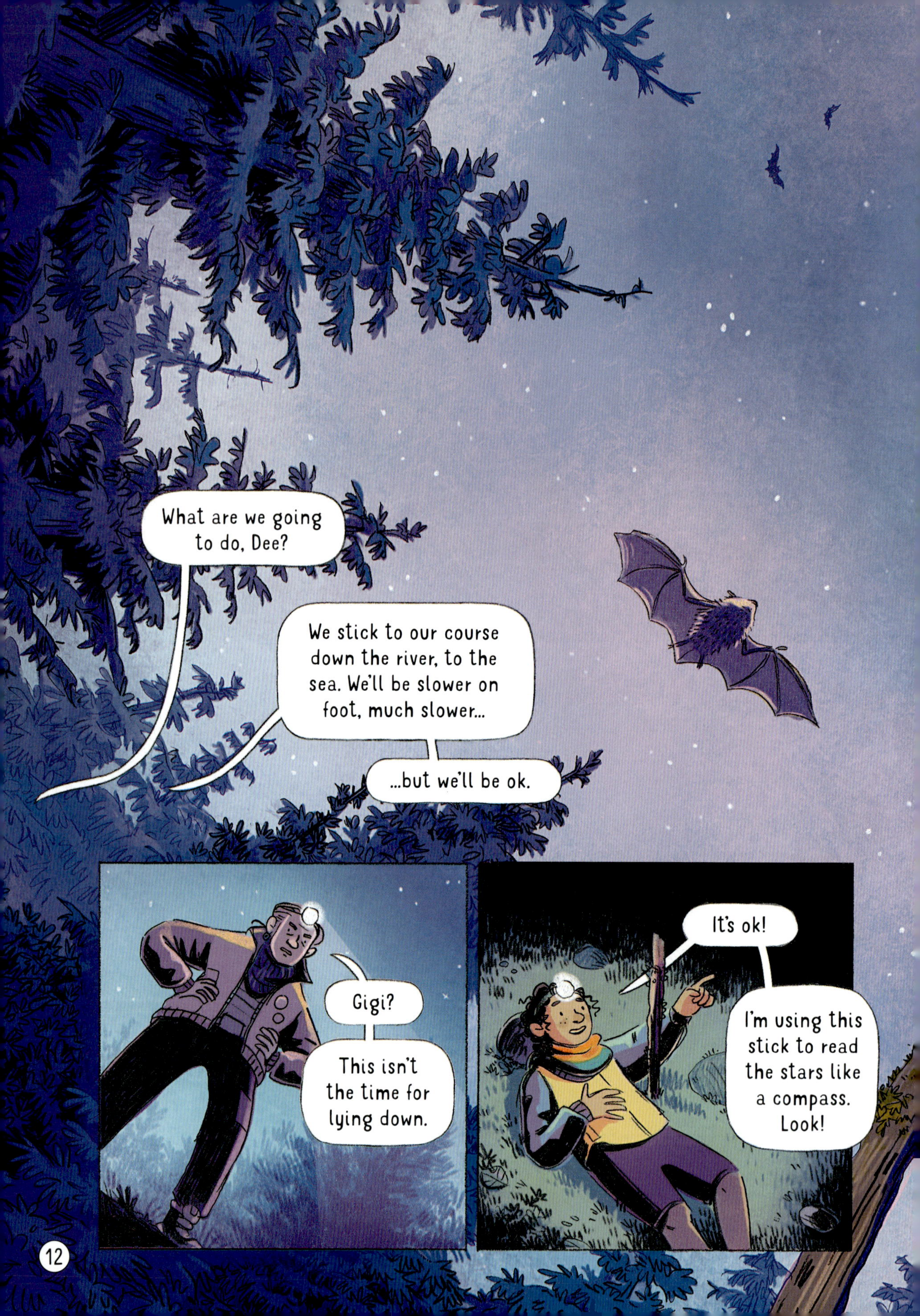
What are we going to do, Dee?
We stick to our course down the river, to the sea. We'll be slower on foot, much slower...
...but we'll be ok.
Gigi?
This isn't the time for lying down.
It's ok!
I'm using this stick to read the stars like a compass. Look!

Navigating with stars

Before compasses were invented, explorers used the stars to guide them. You can use the same tricks to find your way, too.

For this method, you just need a stick planted in the ground. Choose one bright star and watch which way it moves compared to the stick. After about 20 minutes, you'll know which way is which.

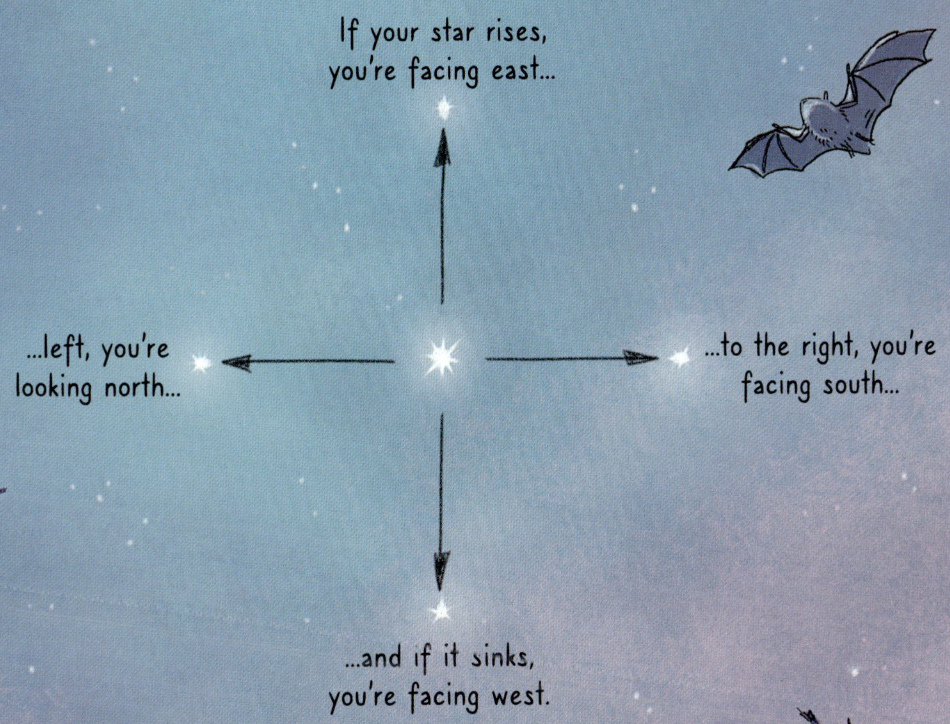

If your star rises, you're facing east...
...left, you're looking north...
...to the right, you're facing south...
...and if it sinks, you're facing west.

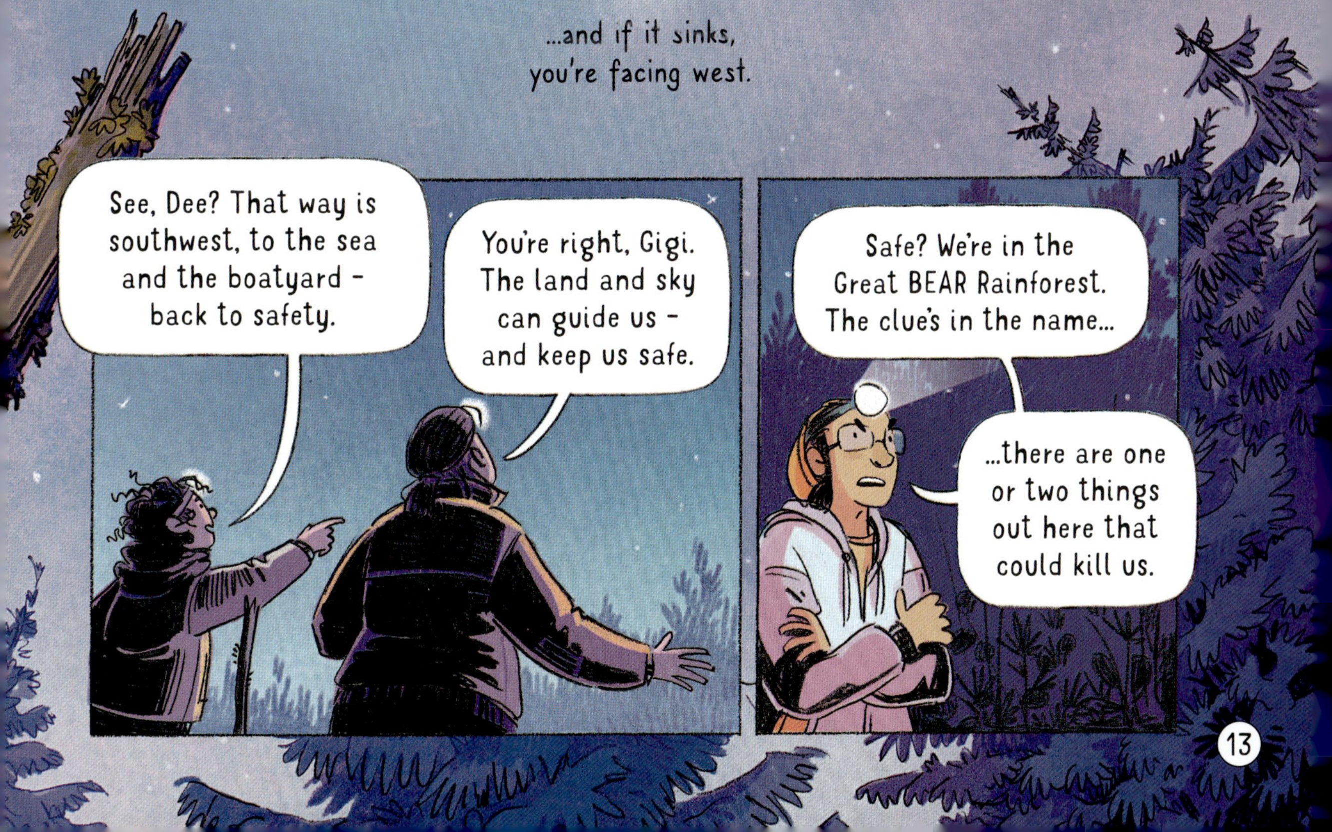

See, Dee? That way is southwest, to the sea and the boatyard - back to safety.
You're right, Gigi. The land and sky can guide us - and keep us safe.
Safe? We're in the Great BEAR Rainforest. The clue's in the name...
...there are one or two things out here that could kill us.

Some animals we don't want to meet...

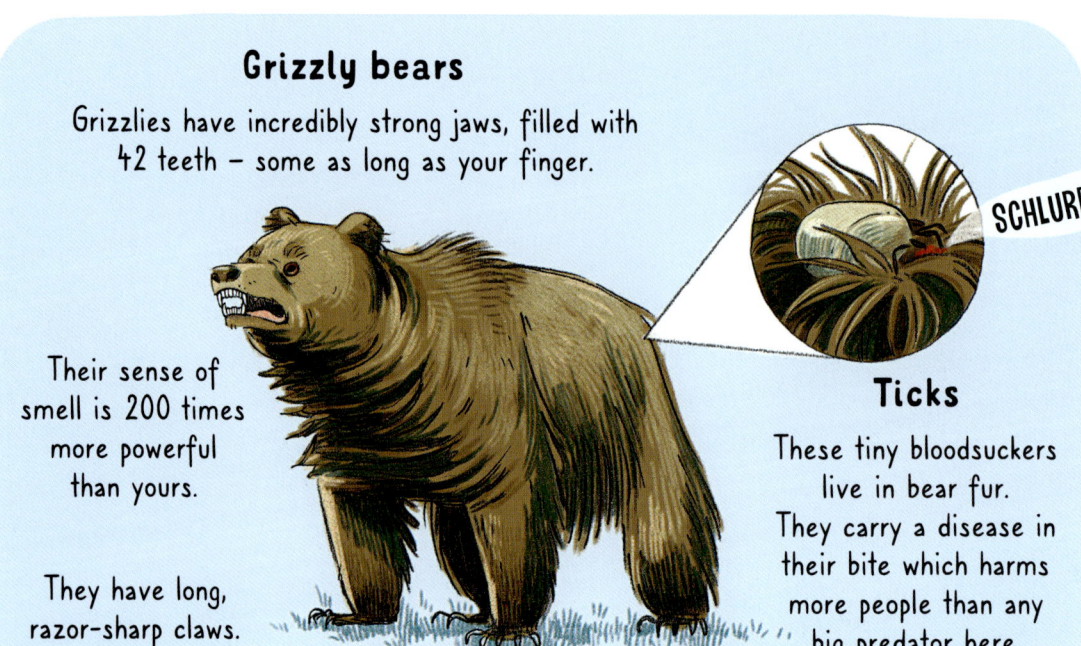

Grizzly bears

Grizzlies have incredibly strong jaws, filled with 42 teeth – some as long as your finger.

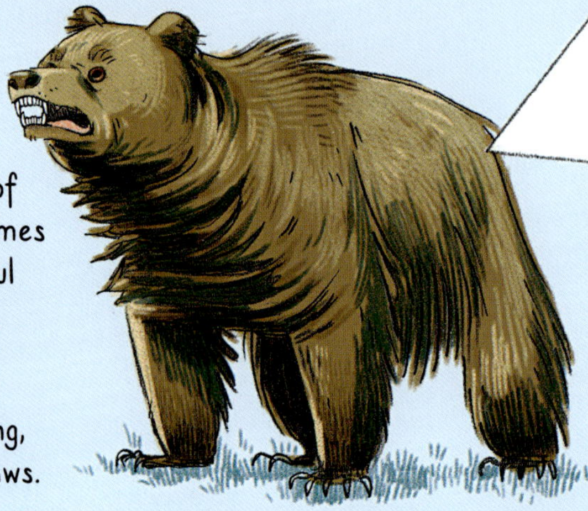

Their sense of smell is 200 times more powerful than yours.

They have long, razor-sharp claws.

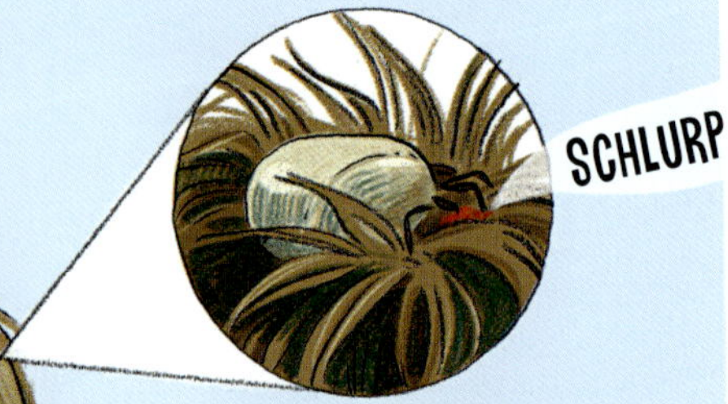
SCHLURP

Ticks

These tiny bloodsuckers live in bear fur. They carry a disease in their bite which harms more people than any big predator here.

Cougars

Cougars stalk their prey for hours in silence – fur and webbed skin on their paws muffle their footsteps.

They don't roar. Their call is a haunting scream.

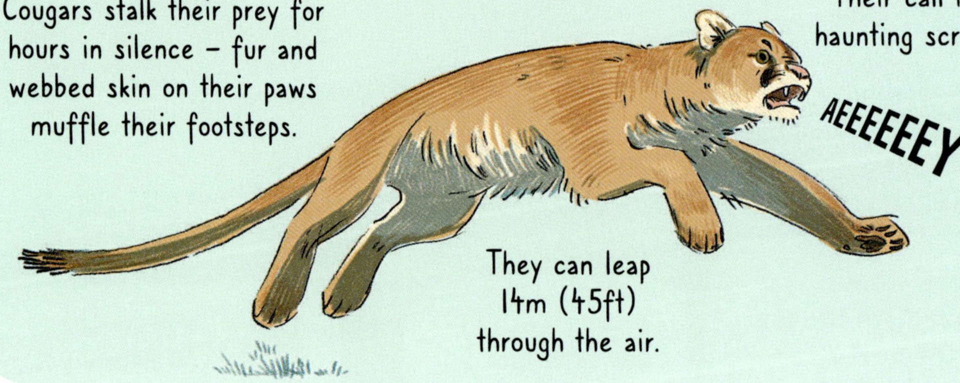
AEEEEEEY

They can leap 14m (45ft) through the air.

Coastal wolves

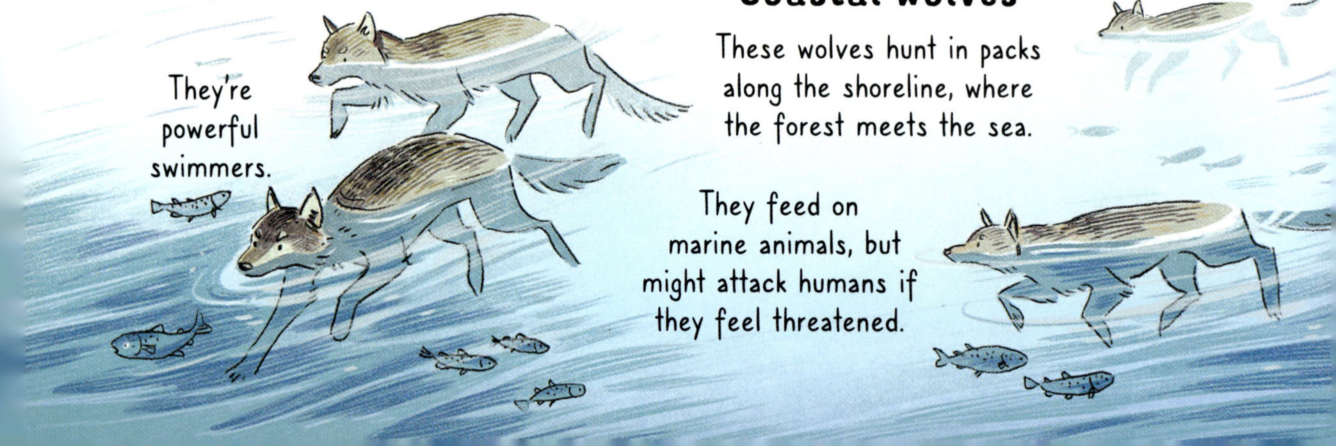

These wolves hunt in packs along the shoreline, where the forest meets the sea.

They're powerful swimmers.

They feed on marine animals, but might attack humans if they feel threatened.

...and what to do if we do

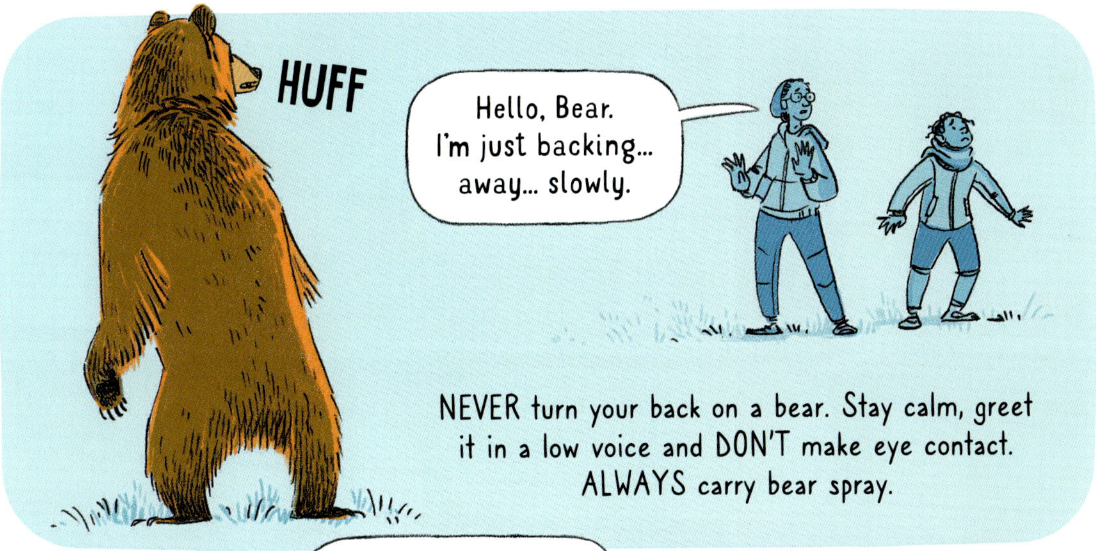
HUFF
Hello, Bear. I'm just backing... away... slowly.
NEVER turn your back on a bear. Stay calm, greet it in a low voice and DON'T make eye contact. ALWAYS carry bear spray.

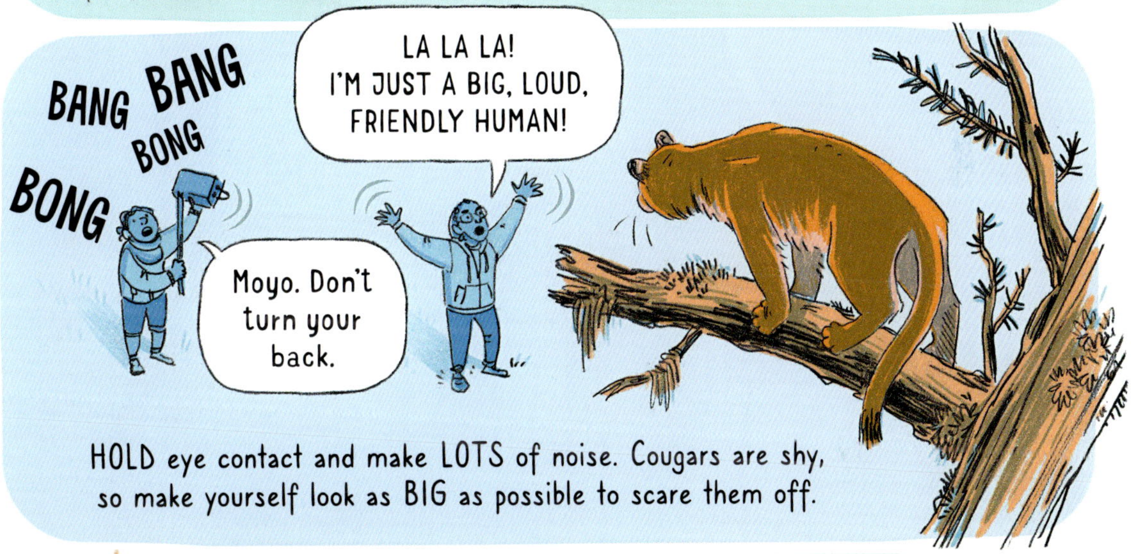
BANG BANG
BONG
BONG
LA LA LA! I'M JUST A BIG, LOUD, FRIENDLY HUMAN!
Moyo. Don't turn your back.
HOLD eye contact and make LOTS of noise. Cougars are shy, so make yourself look as BIG as possible to scare them off.

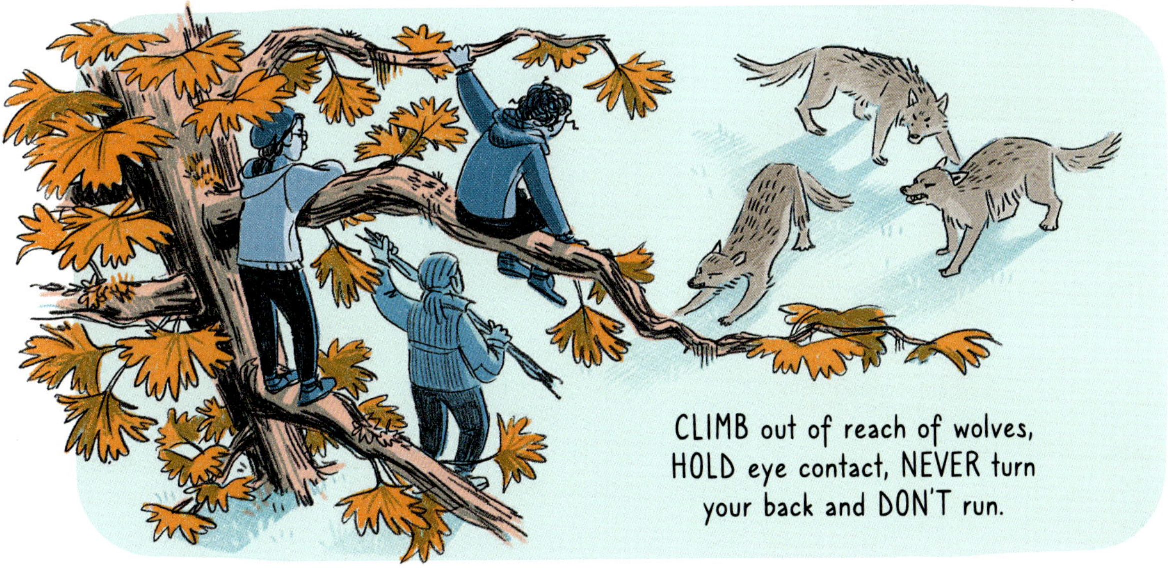
CLIMB out of reach of wolves, HOLD eye contact, NEVER turn your back and DON'T run.

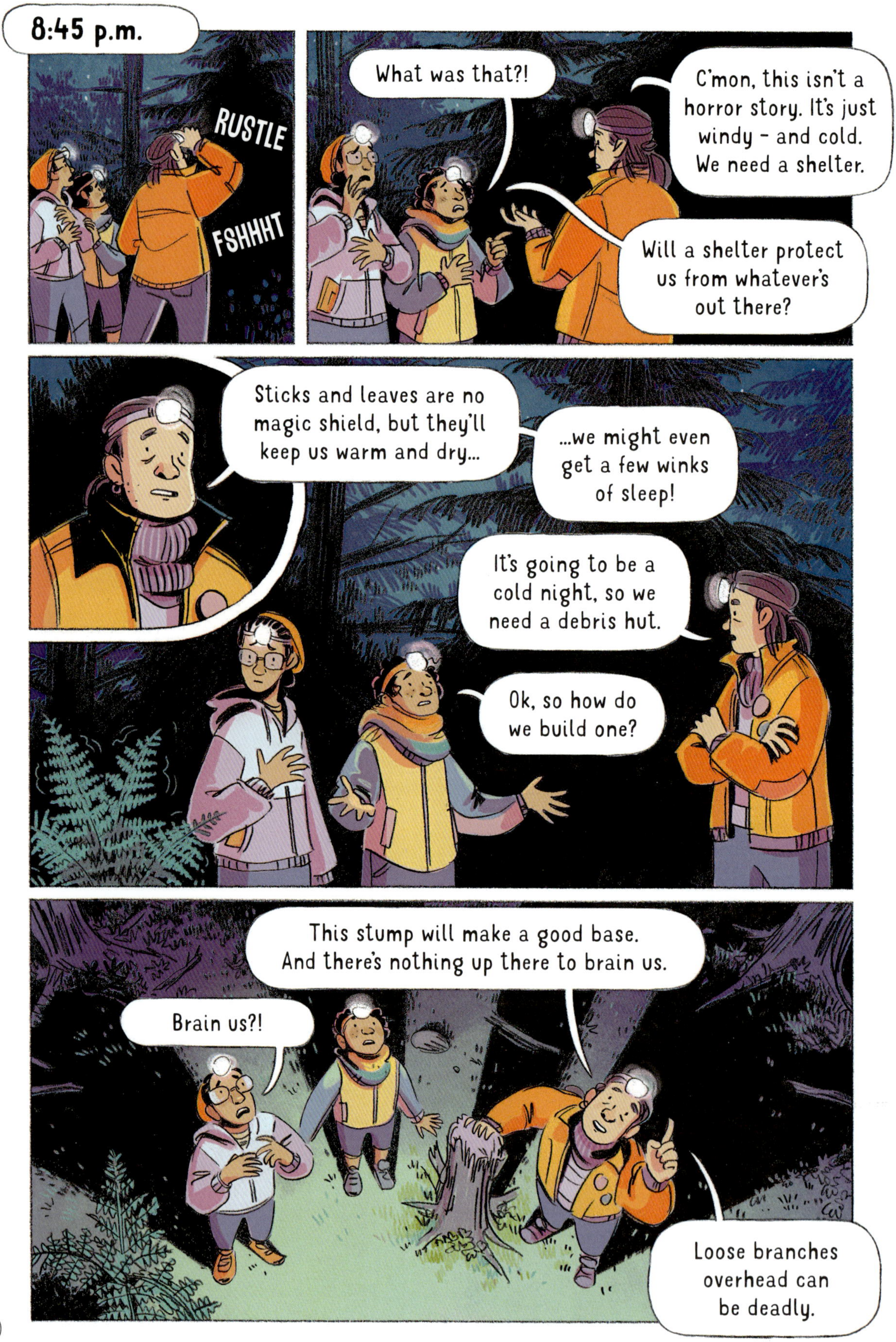
8:45 p.m.
RUSTLE
FSHHHT
What was that?!
C'mon, this isn't a horror story. It's just windy – and cold. We need a shelter.
Will a shelter protect us from whatever's out there?
Sticks and leaves are no magic shield, but they'll keep us warm and dry...
...we might even get a few winks of sleep!
It's going to be a cold night, so we need a debris hut.
Ok, so how do we build one?
This stump will make a good base. And there's nothing up there to brain us.
Brain us?!
Loose branches overhead can be deadly.

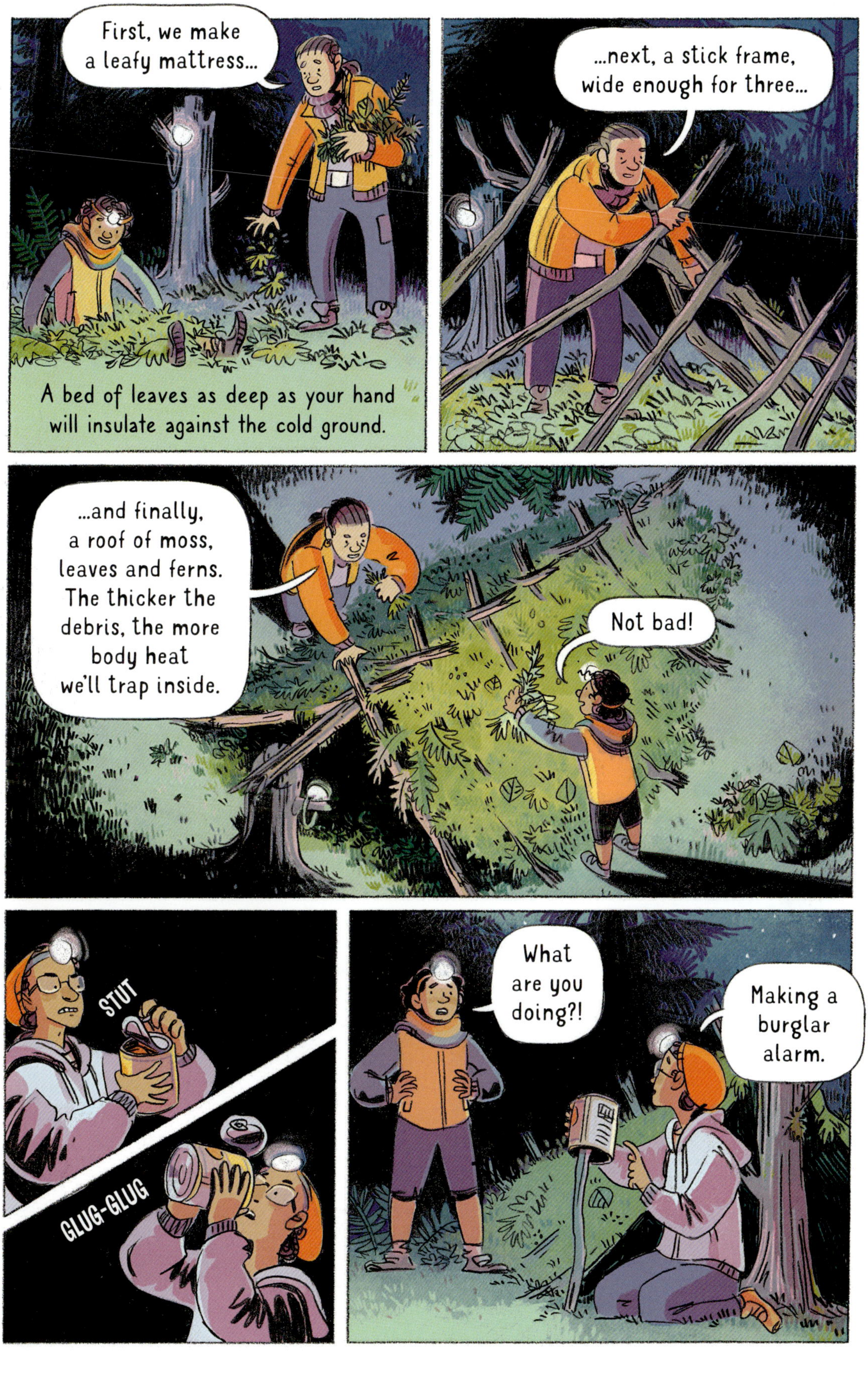

First, we make a leafy mattress...
A bed of leaves as deep as your hand will insulate against the cold ground.
...next, a stick frame, wide enough for three...
...and finally, a roof of moss, leaves and ferns. The thicker the debris, the more body heat we'll trap inside.
Not bad!
STUT
GLUG-GLUG
What are you doing?!
Making a burglar alarm.

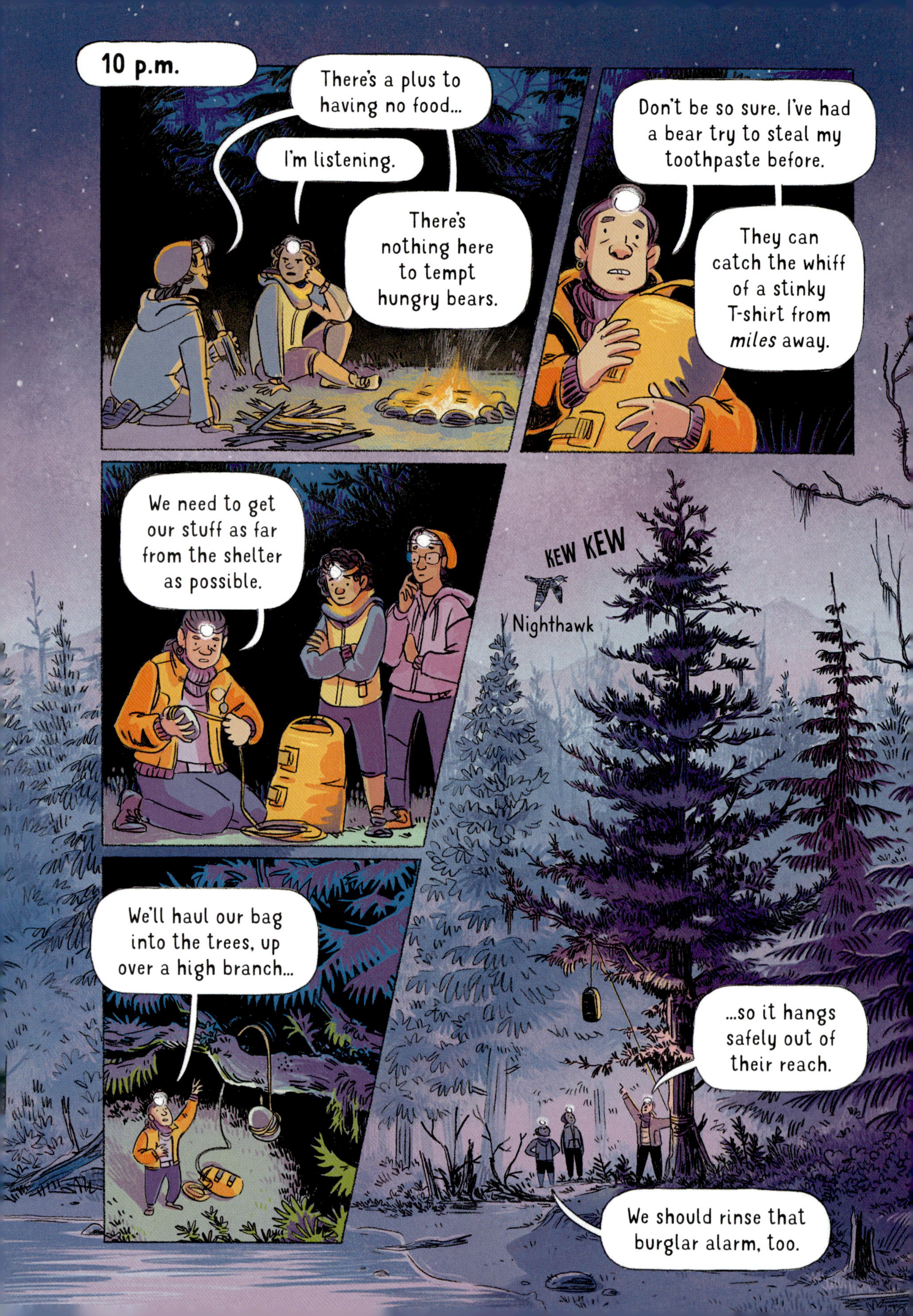
10 p.m.
There's a plus to having no food...
I'm listening.
There's nothing here to tempt hungry bears.
Don't be so sure. I've had a bear try to steal my toothpaste before.
They can catch the whiff of a stinky T-shirt from *miles* away.
We need to get our stuff as far from the shelter as possible.
KEW KEW
Nighthawk
We'll haul our bag into the trees, up over a high branch...
...so it hangs safely out of their reach.
We should rinse that burglar alarm, too.

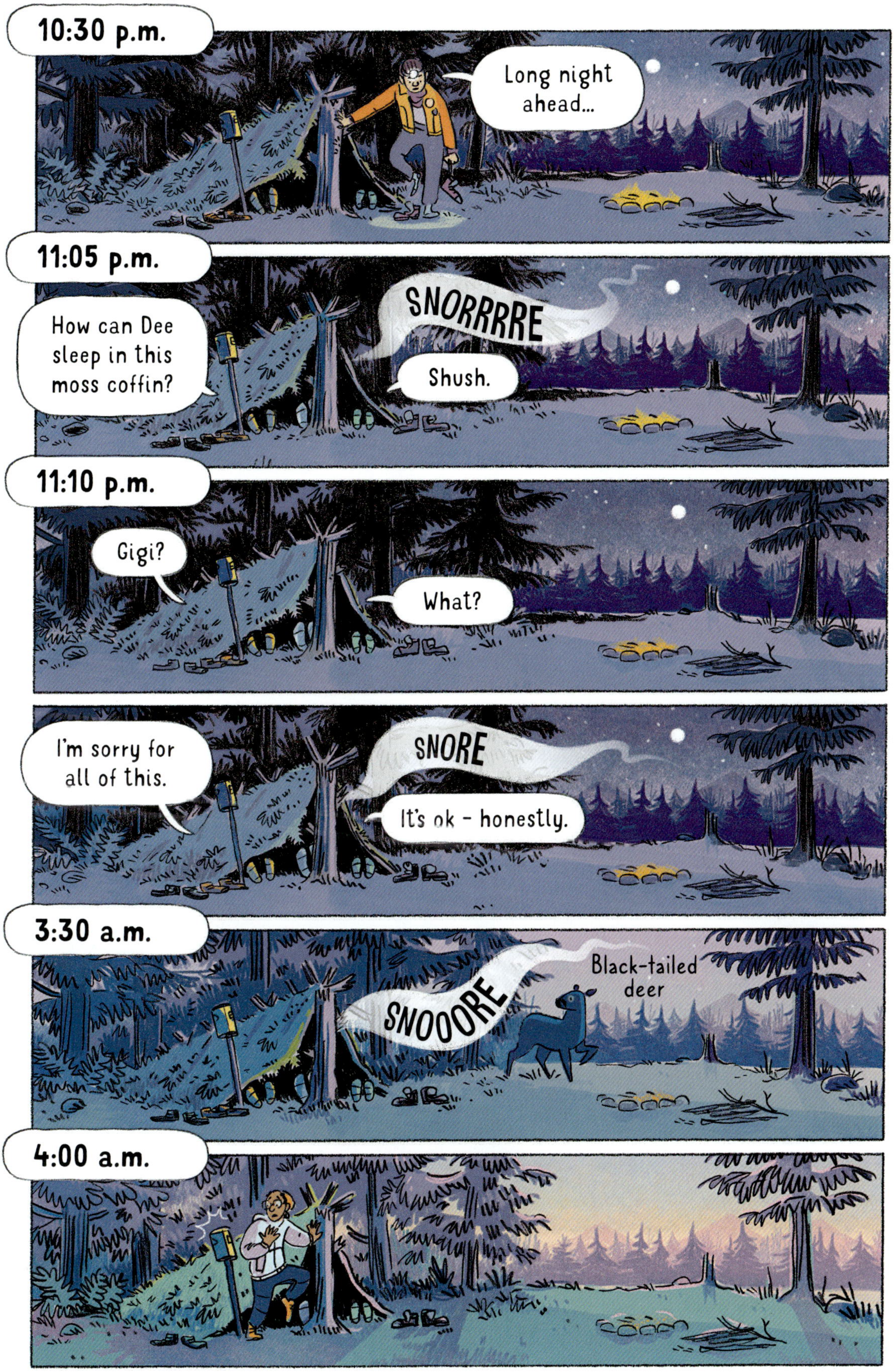
10:30 p.m.
Long night ahead...
11:05 p.m.
How can Dee sleep in this moss coffin?
SNORRRRE
Shush.
11:10 p.m.
Gigi?
What?
I'm sorry for all of this.
SNORE
It's ok - honestly.
3:30 a.m.
SNOOORE
Black-tailed deer
4:00 a.m.

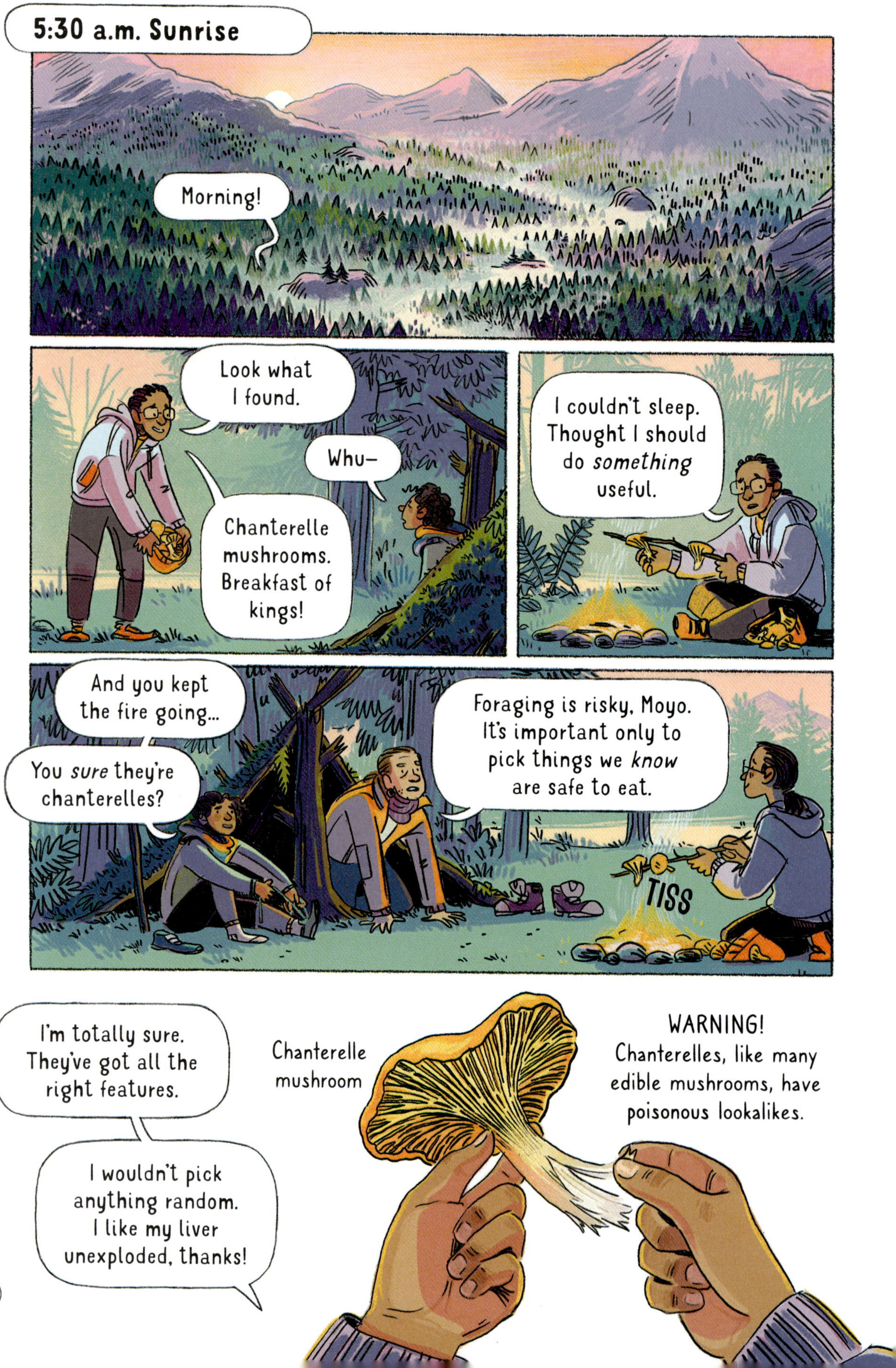
5:30 a.m. Sunrise
Morning!
Look what I found.
Whu–
Chanterelle mushrooms. Breakfast of kings!
I couldn't sleep. Thought I should do *something* useful.
And you kept the fire going...
You *sure* they're chanterelles?
Foraging is risky, Moyo. It's important only to pick things we *know* are safe to eat.
TISS
I'm totally sure. They've got all the right features.
I wouldn't pick anything random. I like my liver unexploded, thanks!
Chanterelle mushroom
WARNING!
Chanterelles, like many edible mushrooms, have poisonous lookalikes.

Forest foraging

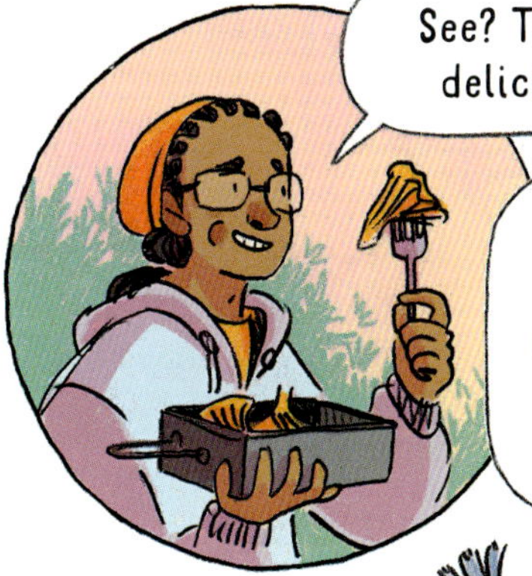
See? They're delicious!
These are some of the wild foods we can look for. I spent a *long* time learning this at forest school!

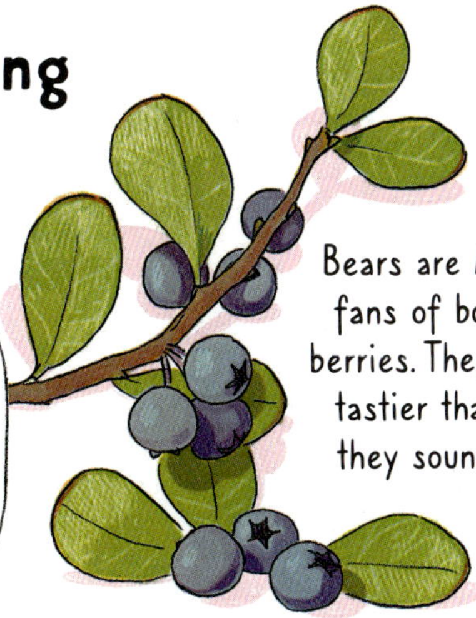

Bears are *big* fans of bog berries. They're tastier than they sound.

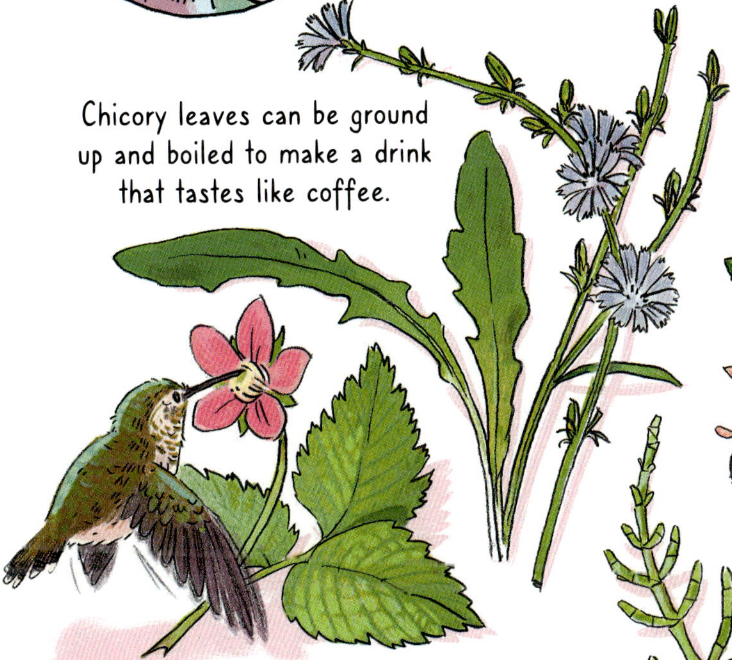

Chicory leaves can be ground up and boiled to make a drink that tastes like coffee.

Fuzzy salal fruits were once plentiful here, but summer droughts have made them rarer.

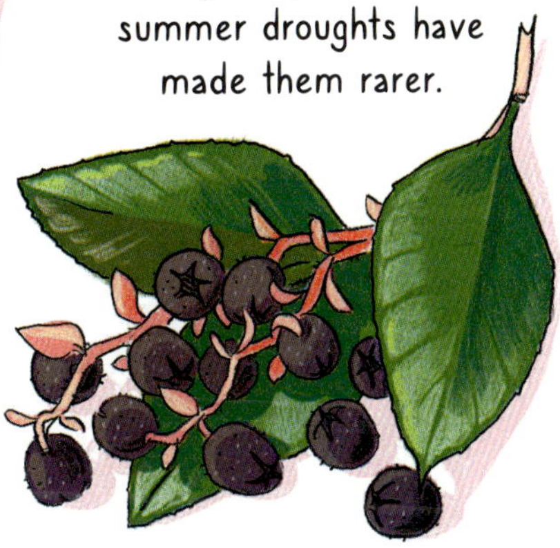

If we make it to the sea, we might find pickleweed. It grows on estuary banks and beaches.

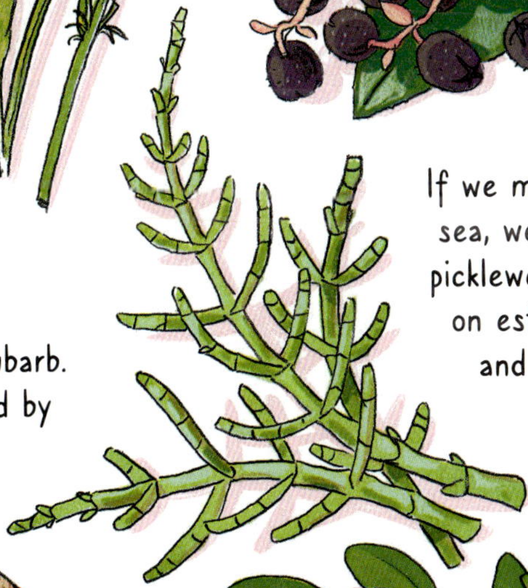

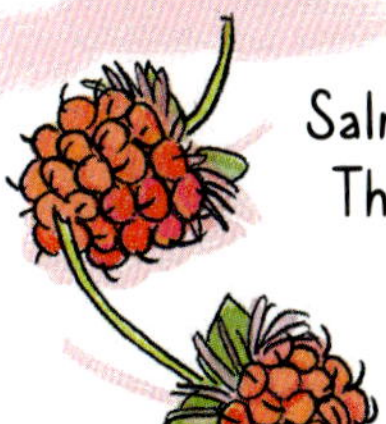

Salmonberries taste like rhubarb. Their flowers are pollinated by tiny hummingbirds.

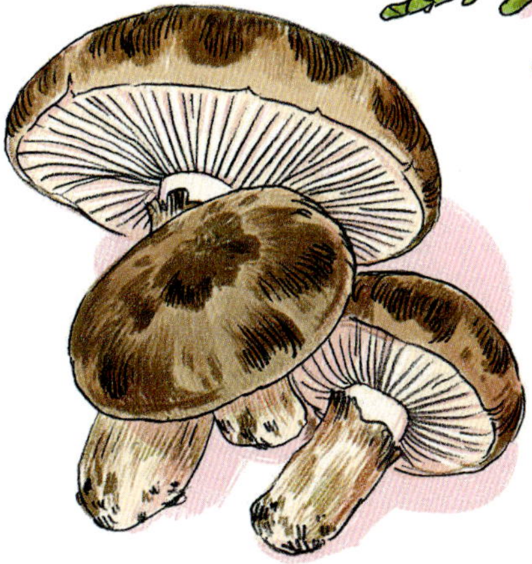

Matsutake are prized by mushroom foragers.

Huckleberries grow in shades of red, blue and purple.

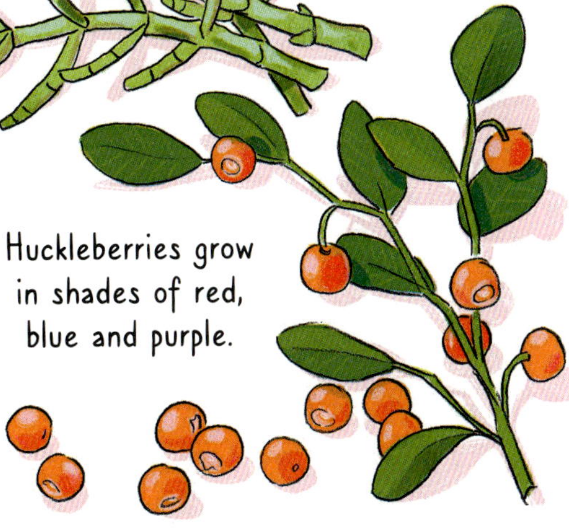

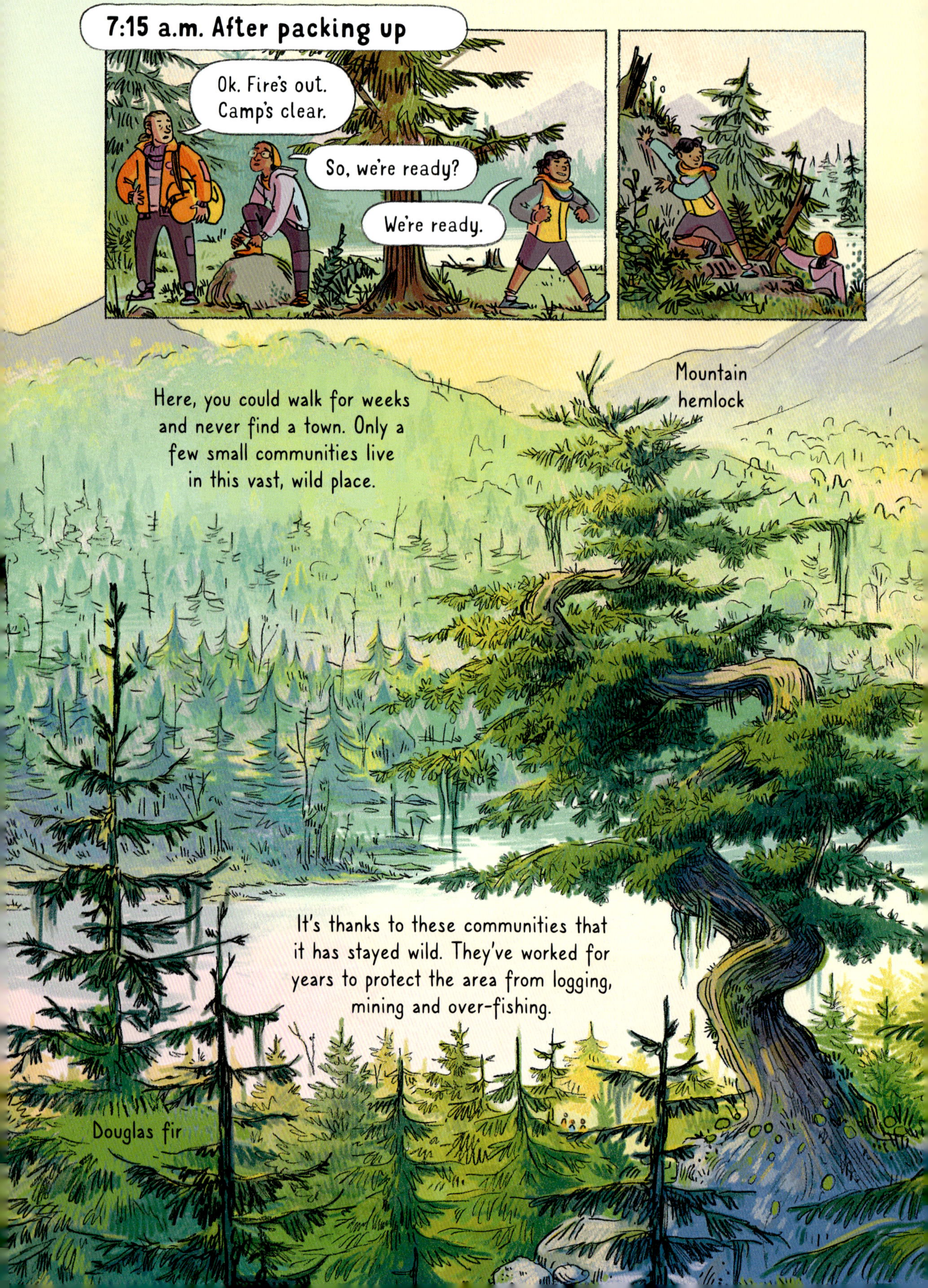

7:15 a.m. After packing up
Ok. Fire's out. Camp's clear.
So, we're ready?
We're ready.
Mountain hemlock
Here, you could walk for weeks and never find a town. Only a few small communities live in this vast, wild place.
It's thanks to these communities that it has stayed wild. They've worked for years to protect the area from logging, mining and over-fishing.
Douglas fir

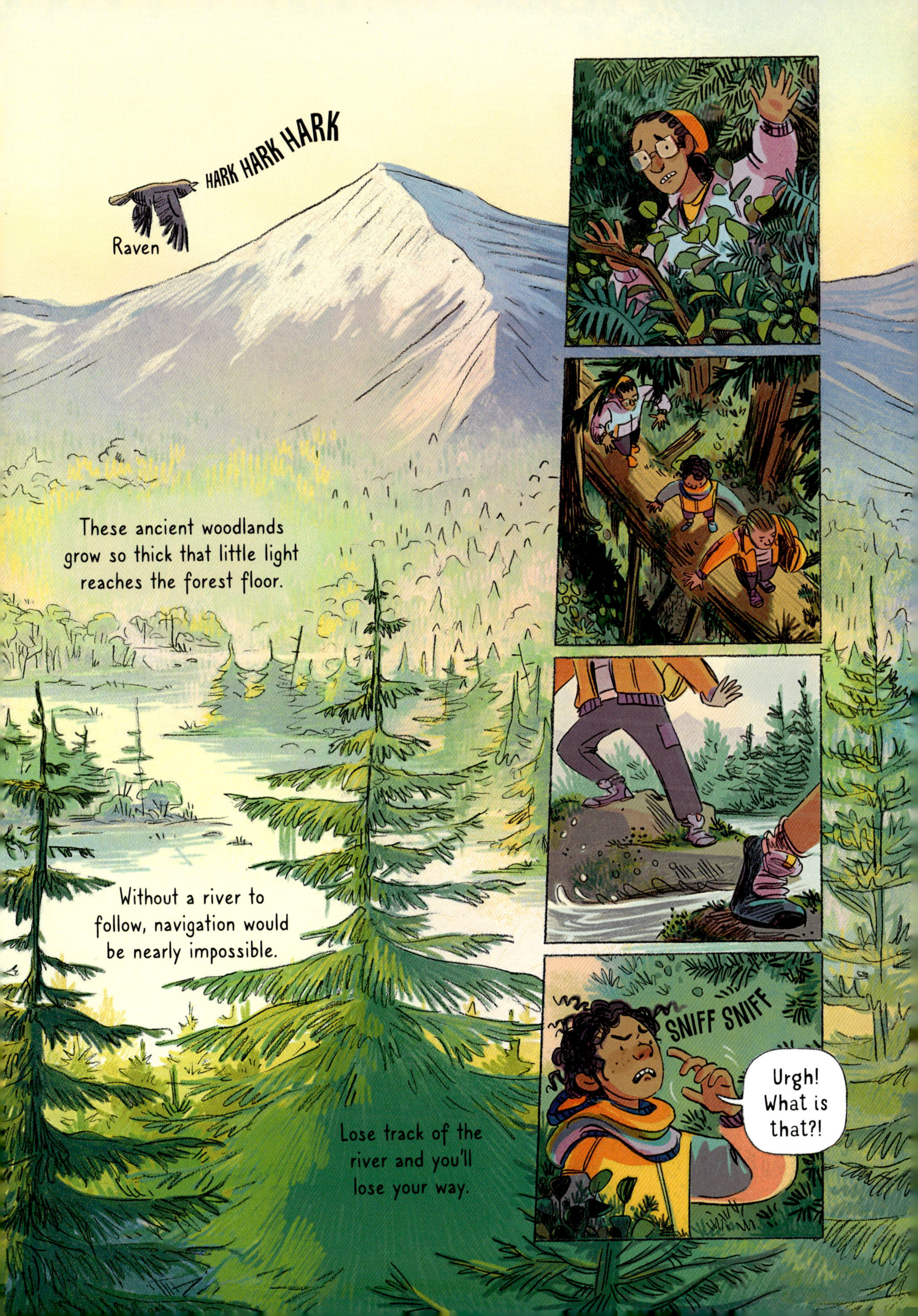
HARK HARK HARK
Raven
These ancient woodlands grow so thick that little light reaches the forest floor.
Without a river to follow, navigation would be nearly impossible.
Lose track of the river and you'll lose your way.
SNIFF SNIFF
Urgh! What is that?!

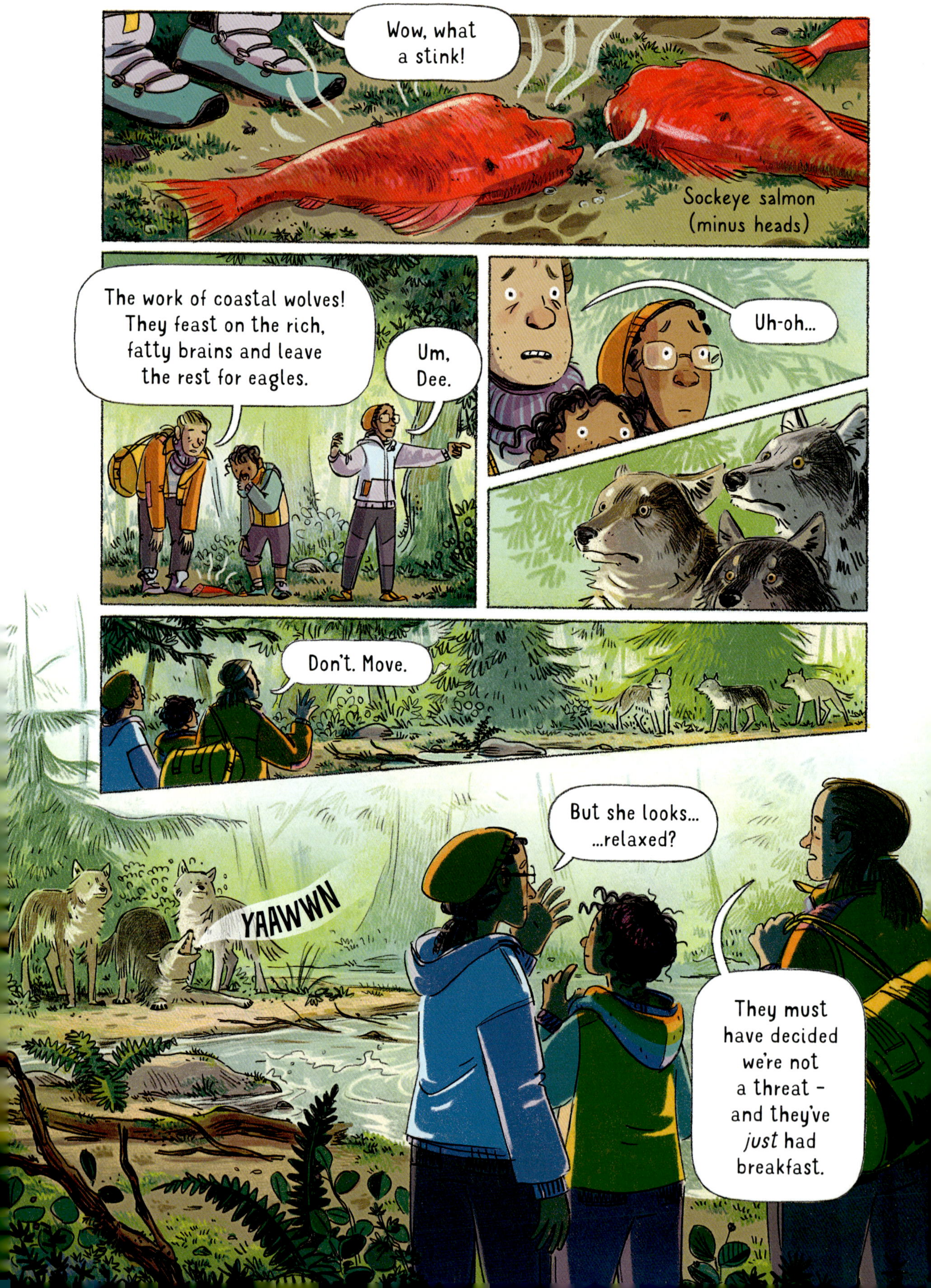
Wow, what a stink!
Sockeye salmon (minus heads)
The work of coastal wolves! They feast on the rich, fatty brains and leave the rest for eagles.
Um, Dee.
Uh-oh...
Don't. Move.
YAAWWN
But she looks... ...relaxed?
They must have decided we're not a threat - and they've *just* had breakfast.

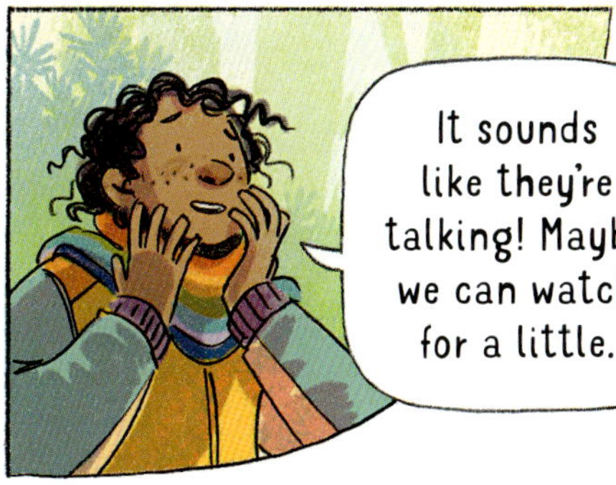
It sounds like they're talking! Maybe we can watch for a little.

How to speak wolf

A wolf pack talks constantly – with barks, growls, whimpers and howls.

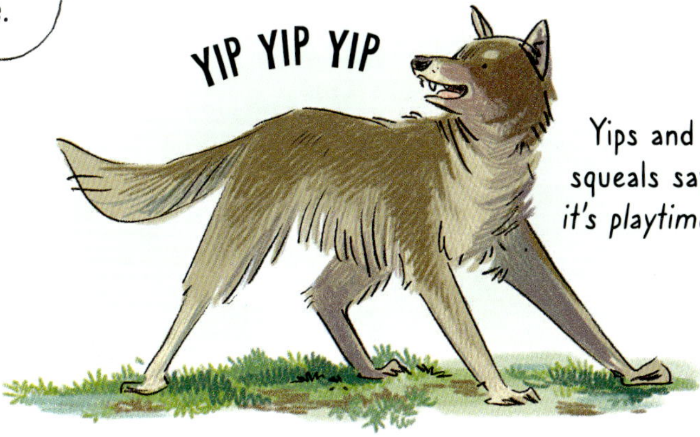
YIP YIP YIP

Yips and squeals say *it's playtime*.

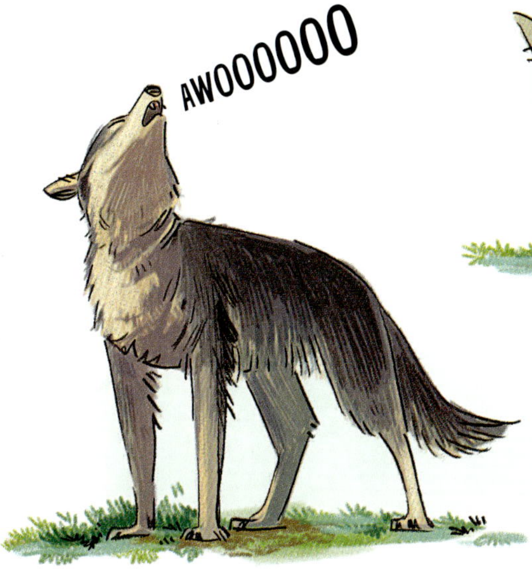
AWOOOOOO

Howls can mean many things. Some draw pack members together. Others tell a rival pack nearby to *back off*.

Wolves also communicate using smelly chemical messages in their dung and urine. Each pack member has its own unique scent.

This helps them keep track of each other, avoid rivals and signal where to find food.

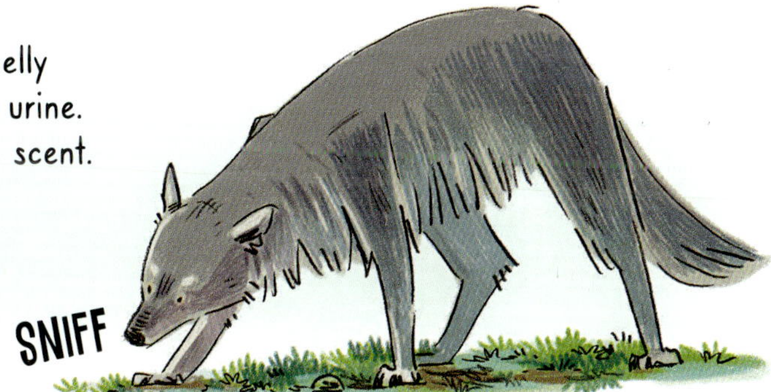
SNIFF

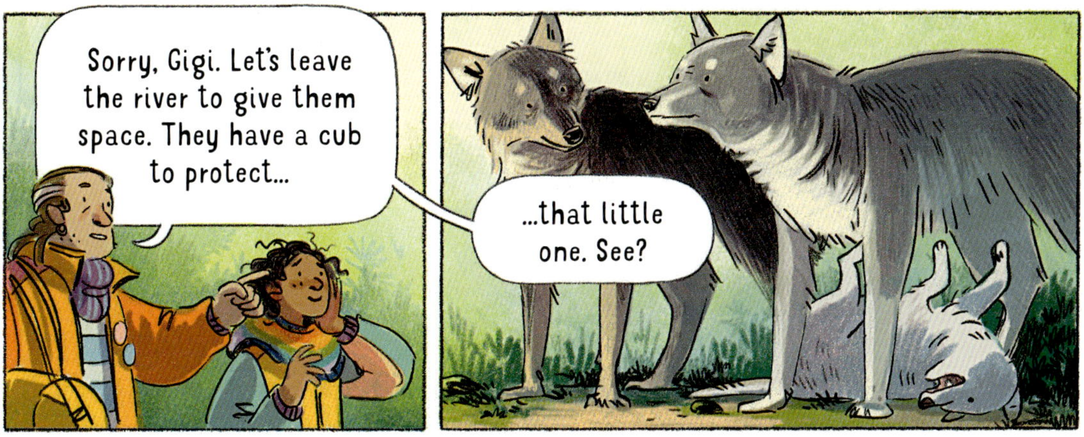
Sorry, Gigi. Let's leave the river to give them space. They have a cub to protect...
...that little one. See?

9:30 a.m. Into the forest

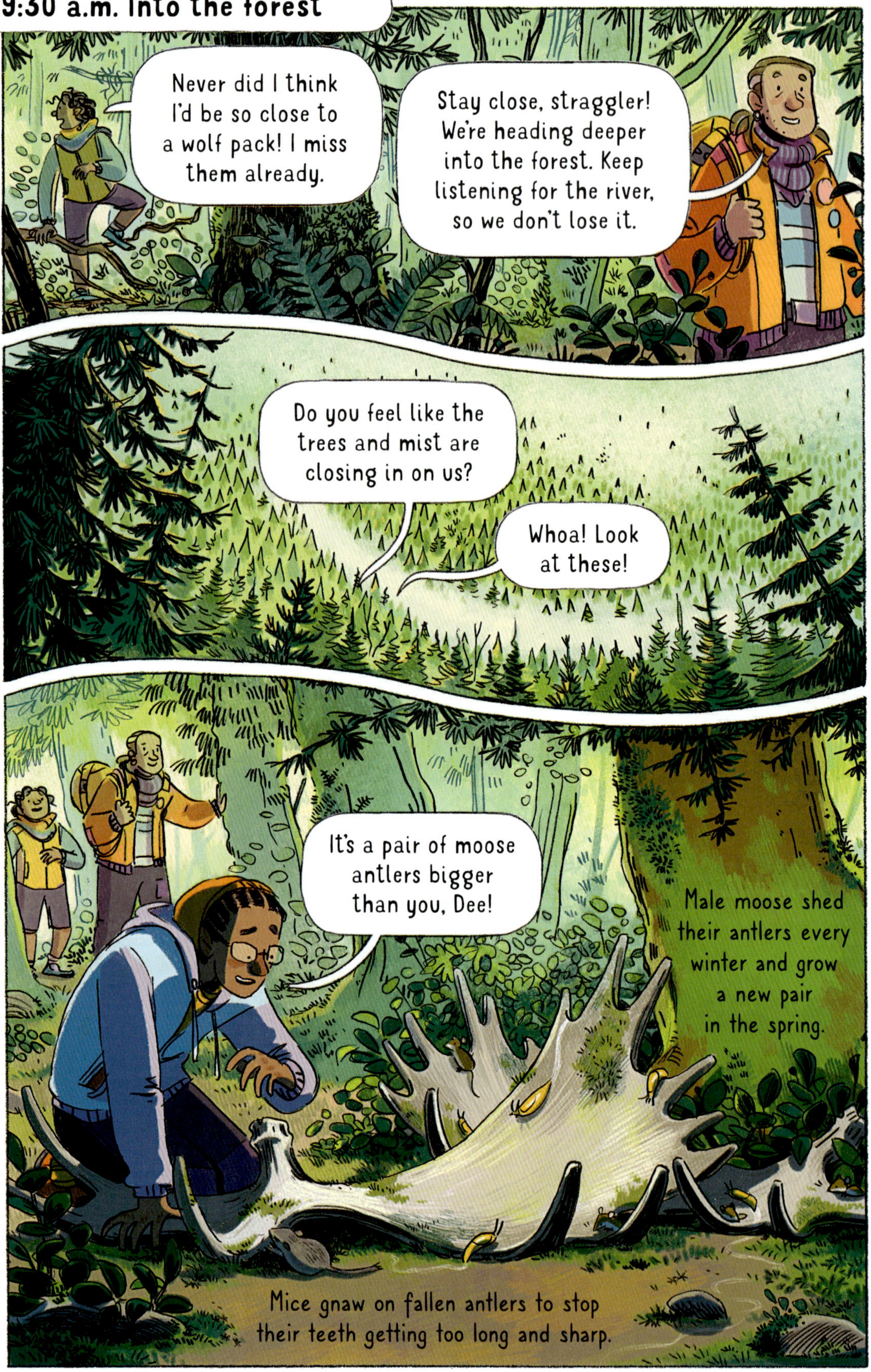
Never did I think I'd be so close to a wolf pack! I miss them already.
Stay close, straggler! We're heading deeper into the forest. Keep listening for the river, so we don't lose it.
Do you feel like the trees and mist are closing in on us?
Whoa! Look at these!
It's a pair of moose antlers bigger than you, Dee!
Male moose shed their antlers every winter and grow a new pair in the spring.
Mice gnaw on fallen antlers to stop their teeth getting too long and sharp.

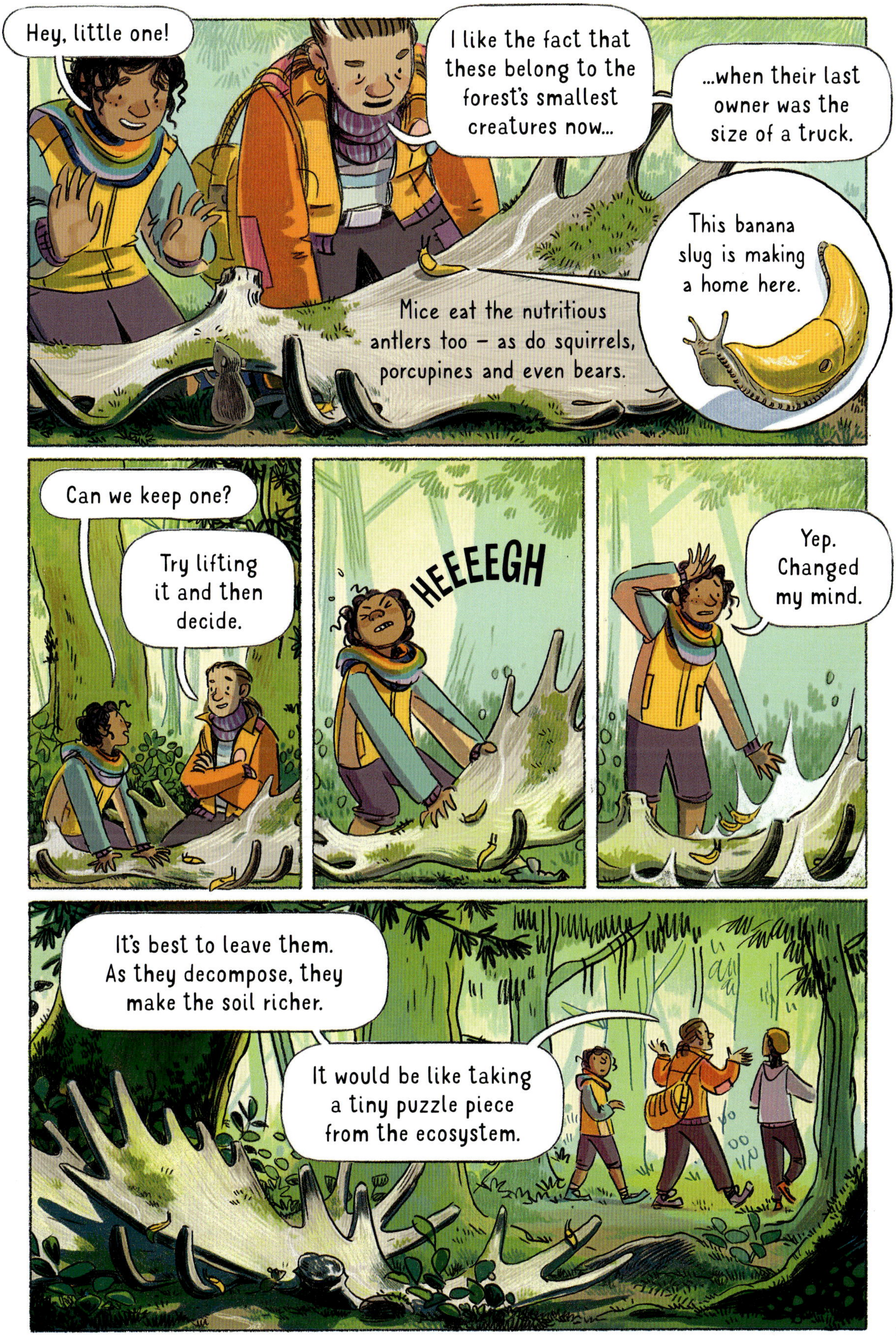
Hey, little one!
I like the fact that these belong to the forest's smallest creatures now...
...when their last owner was the size of a truck.
This banana slug is making a home here.
Mice eat the nutritious antlers too – as do squirrels, porcupines and even bears.
Can we keep one?
Try lifting it and then decide.
HEEEEGH
Yep. Changed my mind.
It's best to leave them. As they decompose, they make the soil richer.
It would be like taking a tiny puzzle piece from the ecosystem.

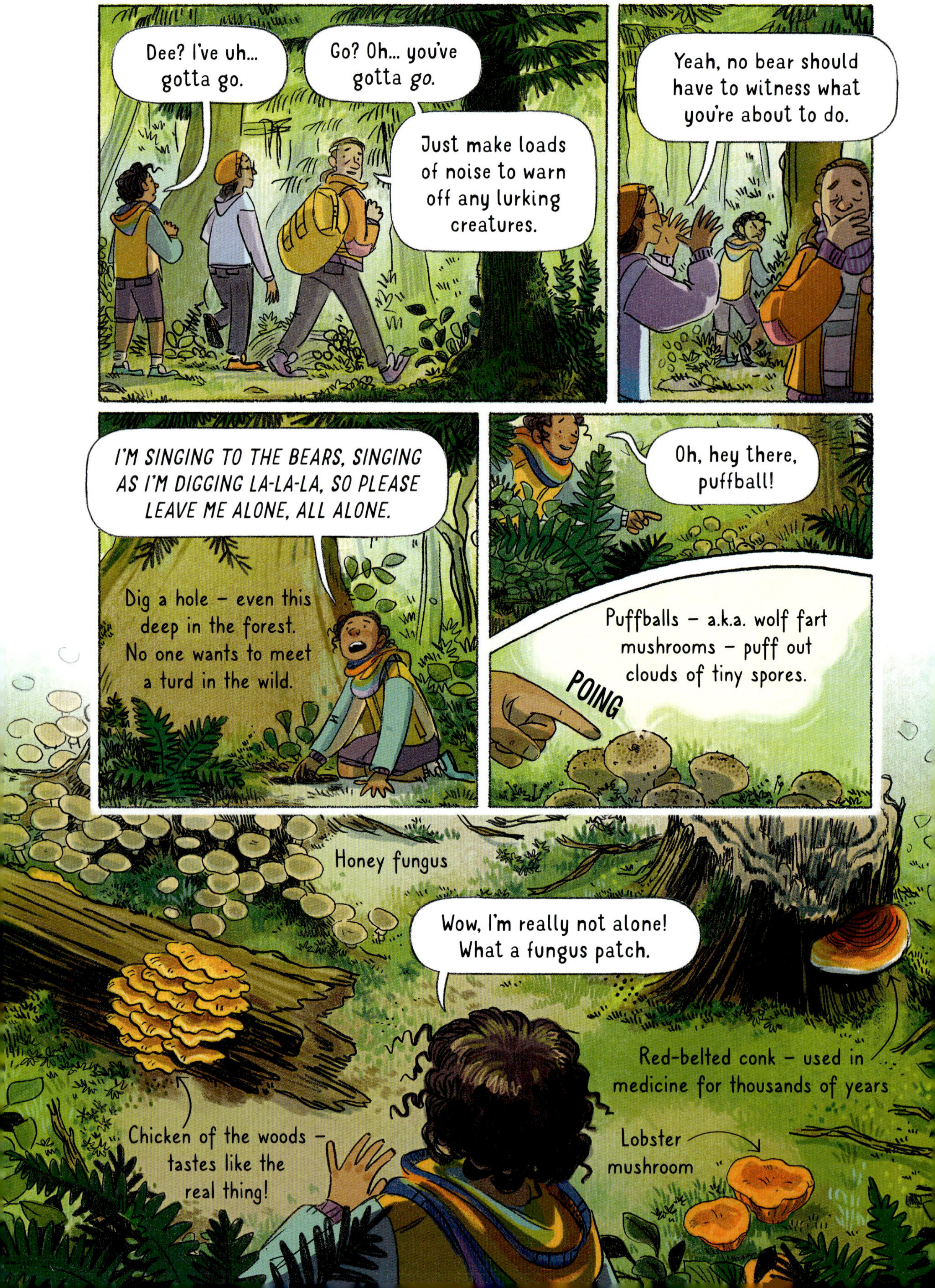
Dee? I've uh... gotta go.
Go? Oh... you've gotta go.
Just make loads of noise to warn off any lurking creatures.
Yeah, no bear should have to witness what you're about to do.
I'M SINGING TO THE BEARS, SINGING AS I'M DIGGING LA-LA-LA, SO PLEASE LEAVE ME ALONE, ALL ALONE.
Dig a hole – even this deep in the forest. No one wants to meet a turd in the wild.
Oh, hey there, puffball!
Puffballs – a.k.a. wolf fart mushrooms – puff out clouds of tiny spores.
POING
Honey fungus
Wow, I'm really not alone! What a fungus patch.
Red-belted conk – used in medicine for thousands of years
Chicken of the woods – tastes like the real thing!
Lobster mushroom

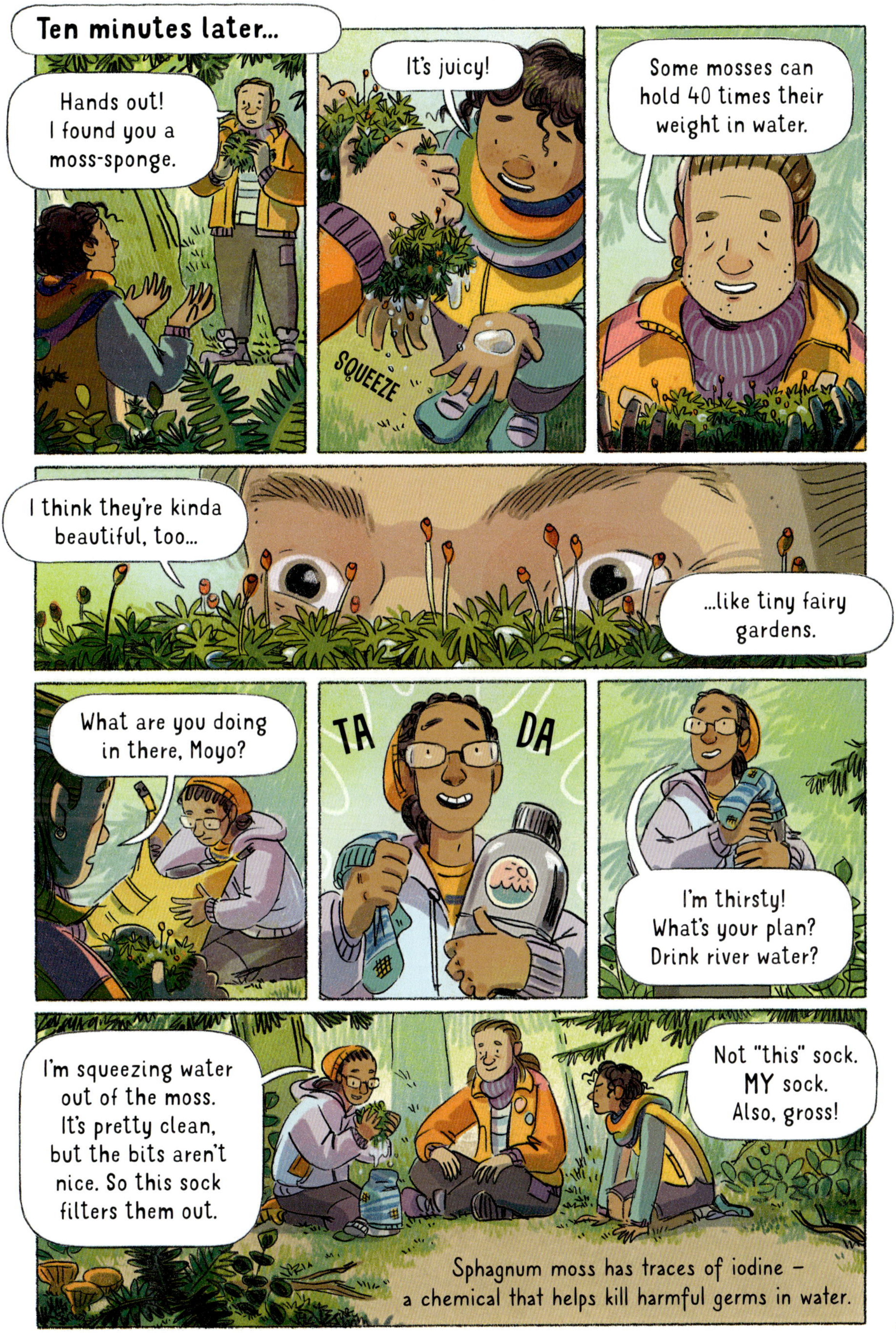
Ten minutes later...
Hands out! I found you a moss-sponge.
It's juicy!
SQUEEZE
Some mosses can hold 40 times their weight in water.
I think they're kinda beautiful, too...
...like tiny fairy gardens.
What are you doing in there, Moyo?
TA
DA
I'm thirsty! What's your plan? Drink river water?
I'm squeezing water out of the moss. It's pretty clean, but the bits aren't nice. So this sock filters them out.
Not "this" sock. MY sock. Also, gross!
Sphagnum moss has traces of iodine – a chemical that helps kill harmful germs in water.

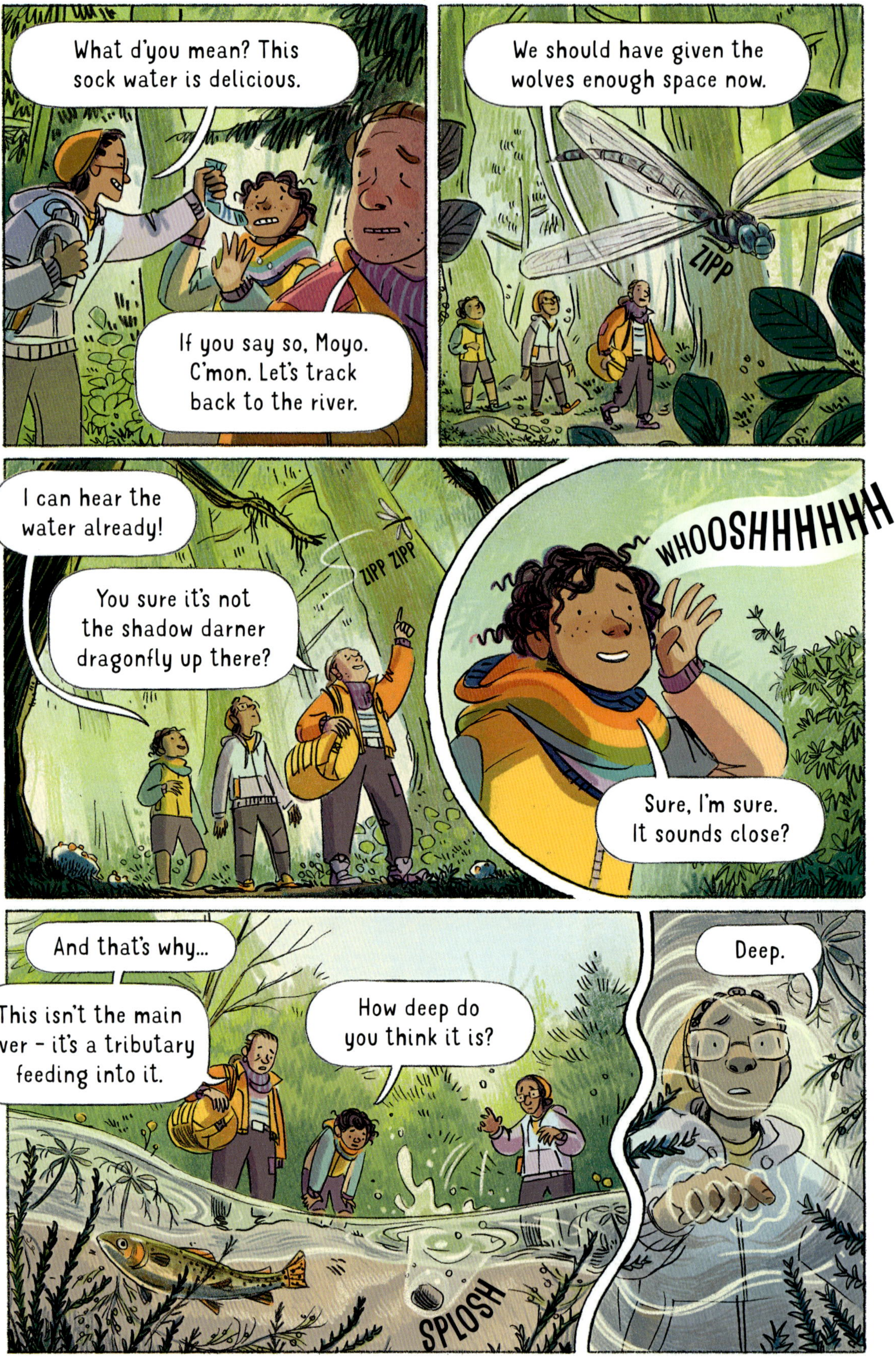
What d'you mean? This sock water is delicious.
If you say so, Moyo. C'mon. Let's track back to the river.
We should have given the wolves enough space now.
ZIPP
I can hear the water already!
ZIPP ZIPP
You sure it's not the shadow darner dragonfly up there?
WHOOSHHHHHH
Sure, I'm sure. It sounds close?
And that's why...
This isn't the main river – it's a tributary feeding into it.
How deep do you think it is?
SPLOSH
Deep.

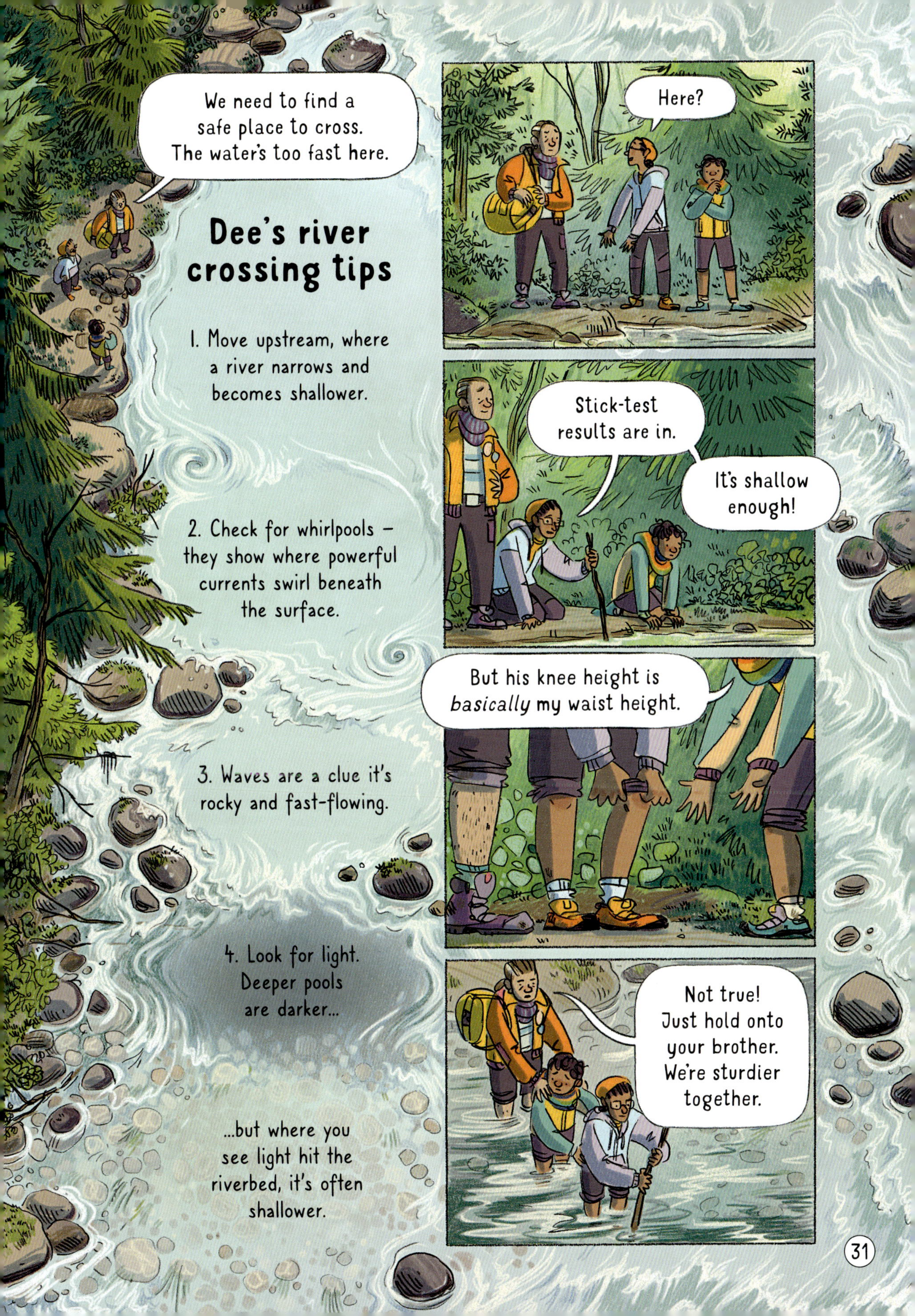
We need to find a safe place to cross. The water's too fast here.
Here?
Dee's river crossing tips
1. Move upstream, where a river narrows and becomes shallower.
Stick-test results are in.
It's shallow enough!
2. Check for whirlpools – they show where powerful currents swirl beneath the surface.
But his knee height is *basically* my waist height.
3. Waves are a clue it's rocky and fast-flowing.
4. Look for light. Deeper pools are darker...
Not true! Just hold onto your brother. We're sturdier together.
...but where you see light hit the riverbed, it's often shallower.

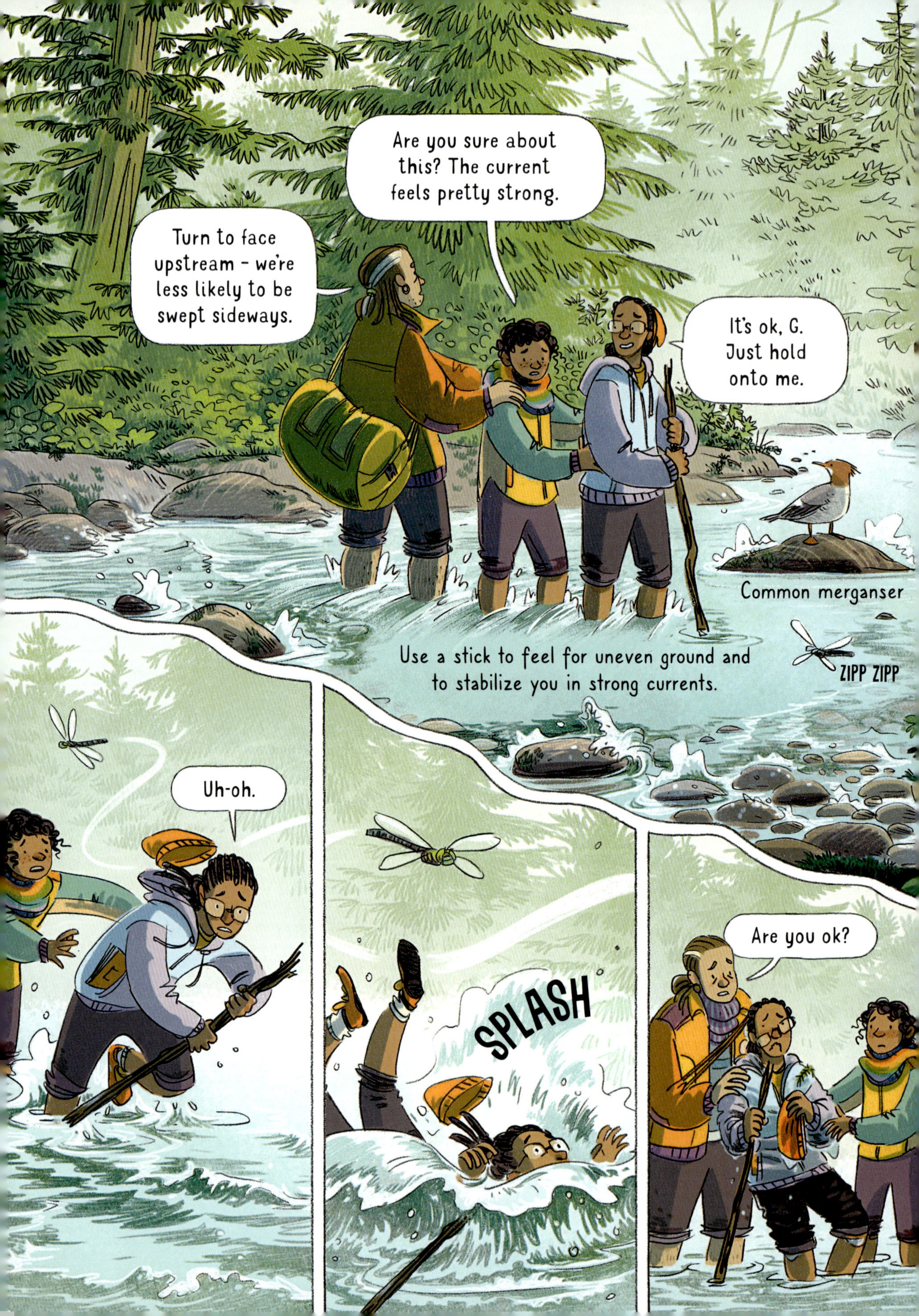

Are you sure about this? The current feels pretty strong.
Turn to face upstream - we're less likely to be swept sideways.
It's ok, G. Just hold onto me.
Common merganser
Use a stick to feel for uneven ground and to stabilize you in strong currents.
ZIPP ZIPP
Uh-oh.
SPLASH
Are you ok?

No cuts? No bangs?
I'm fine, honestly. Just wet.
And cold.
Take off your wet things and put this on.
We don't want you getting hypothermia.

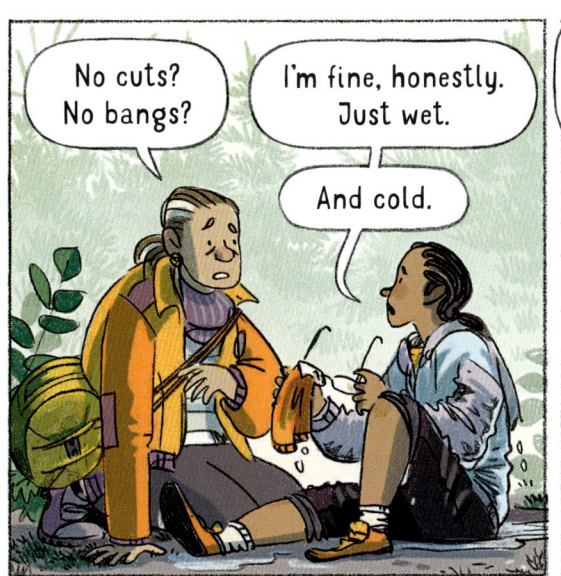

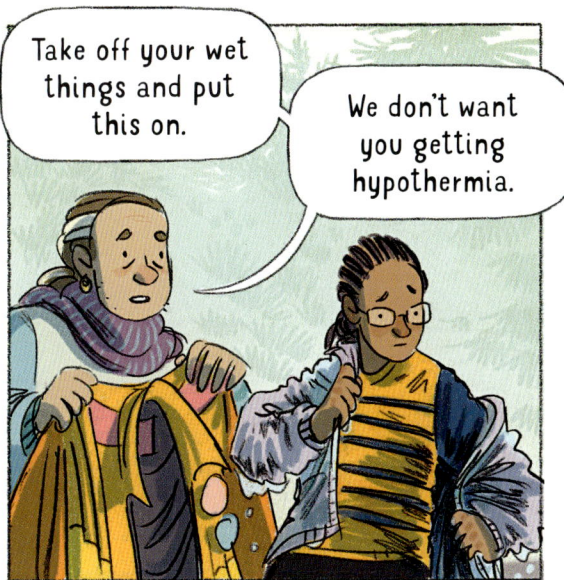

Hypothermia – and how to stop it

Being very cold can lead to a condition called hypothermia. This is the number one killer in the wilderness – bigger than hunger or animal attacks. So act fast if someone is showing any of these tell-tale signs:

unstoppable shivering, drowsiness, slurred speech or confusion.

Here's what to do for someone at risk:

1. Wrap them up in something warm and dry, taking off any wet clothes first.

2. Light a fire nearby, but not too close. If they warm up too fast, they could go into shock.

3. Heat water over the fire and carefully pour it into a metal bottle. Wrapped in a shirt, this works like a hot water bottle.

4. Find or make a shelter to protect them from the elements.

5. Keep an eye on their vital signs – feel their pulse and check they're breathing normally.

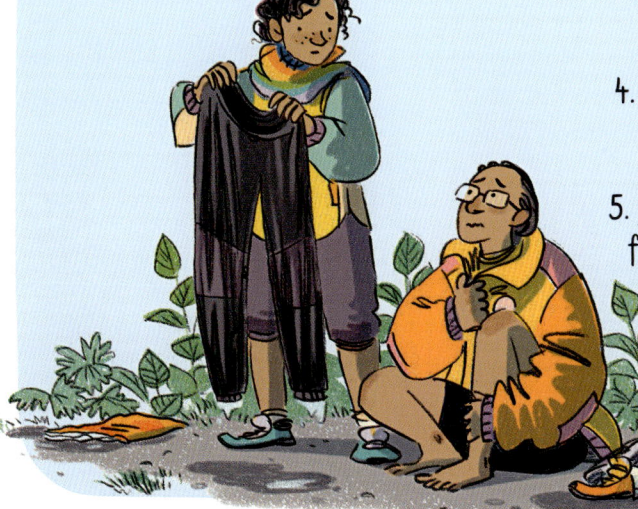

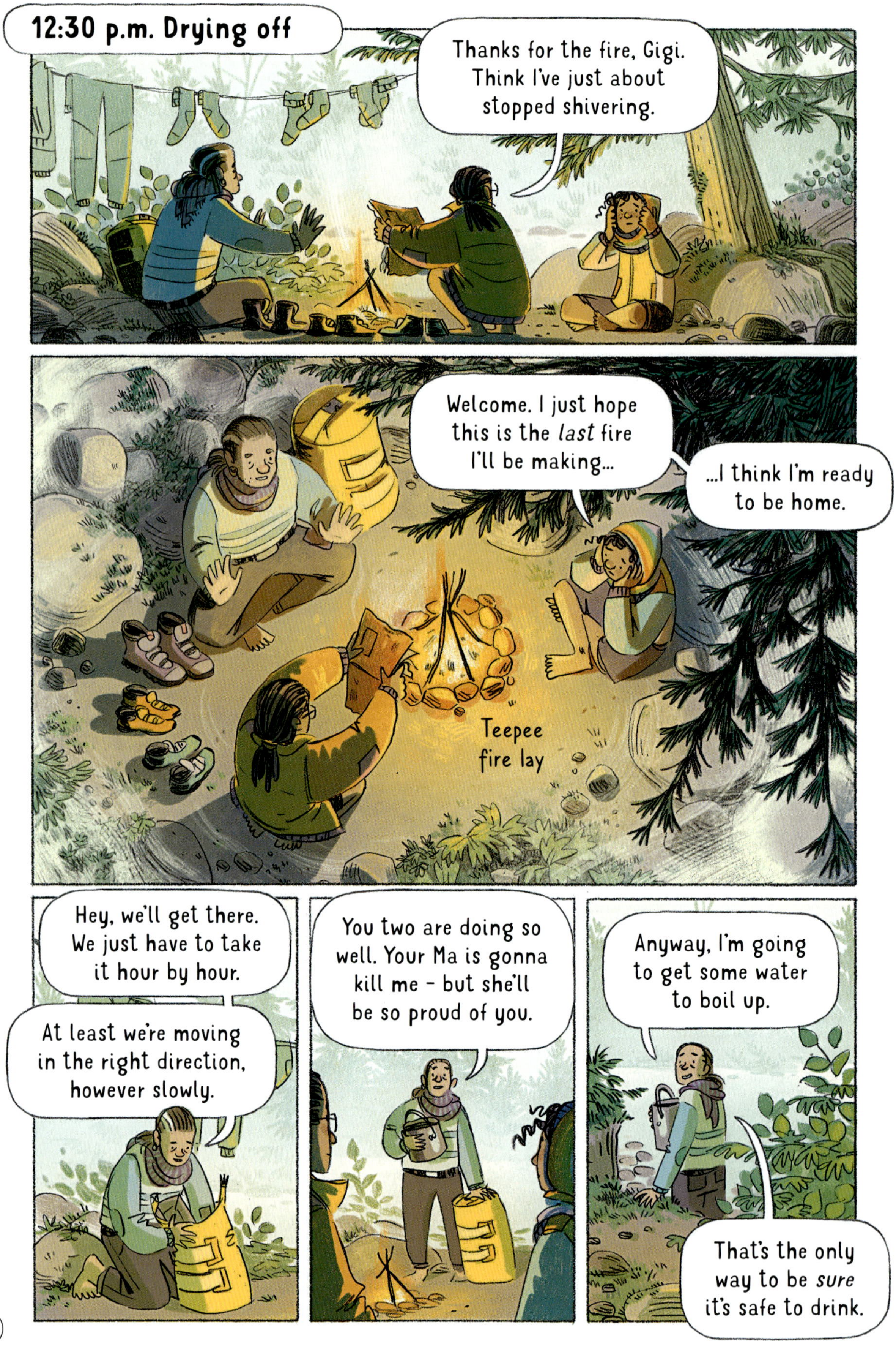
12:30 p.m. Drying off
Thanks for the fire, Gigi. Think I've just about stopped shivering.
Welcome. I just hope this is the *last* fire I'll be making...
...I think I'm ready to be home.
Teepee fire lay
Hey, we'll get there. We just have to take it hour by hour.
At least we're moving in the right direction, however slowly.
You two are doing so well. Your Ma is gonna kill me – but she'll be so proud of you.
Anyway, I'm going to get some water to boil up.
That's the only way to be *sure* it's safe to drink.

At the water's edge

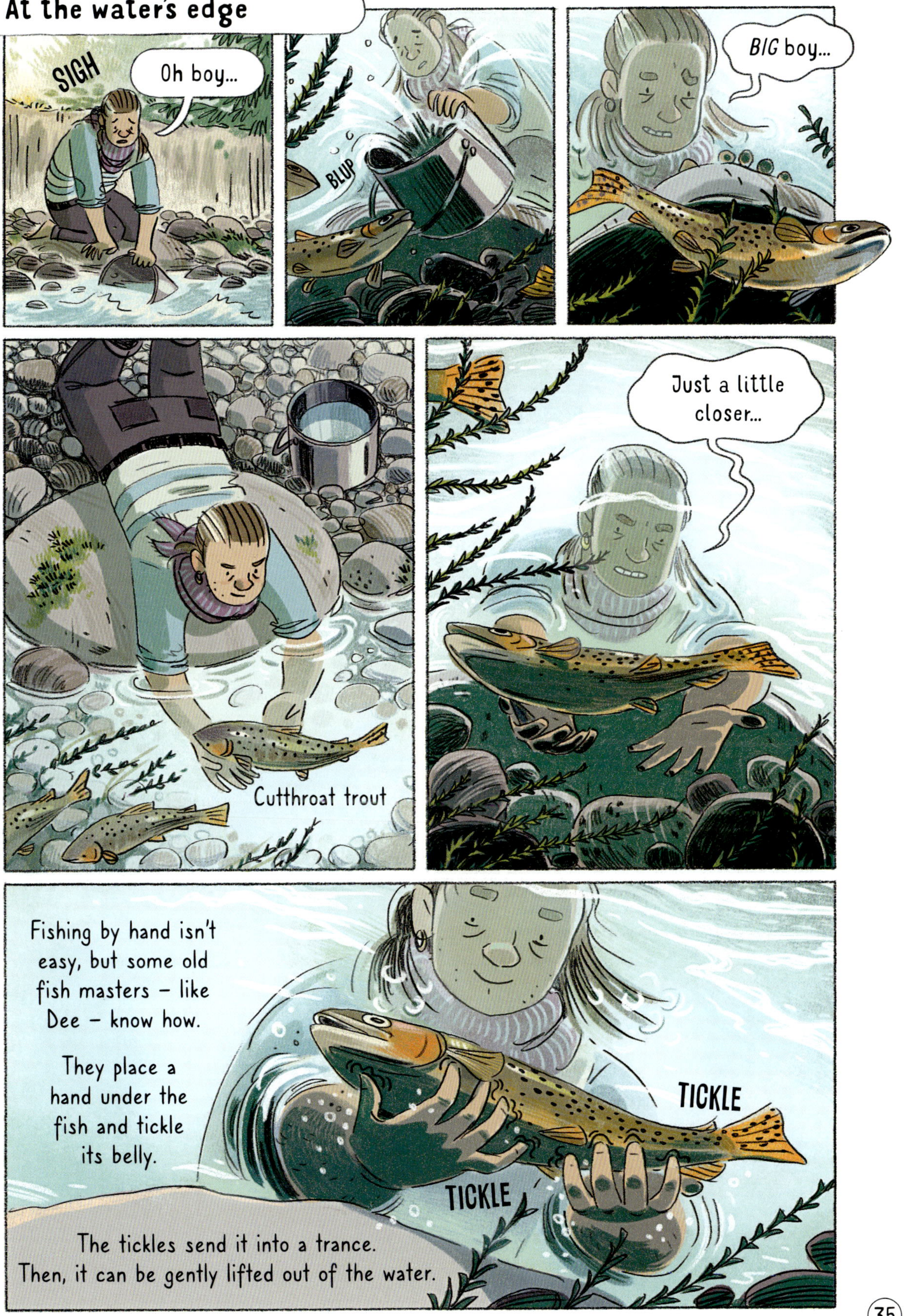
SIGH
Oh boy...
BLUP
BIG boy...
Cutthroat trout
Just a little closer...
Fishing by hand isn't easy, but some old fish masters – like Dee – know how.
They place a hand under the fish and tickle its belly.
TICKLE
TICKLE
The tickles send it into a trance. Then, it can be gently lifted out of the water.

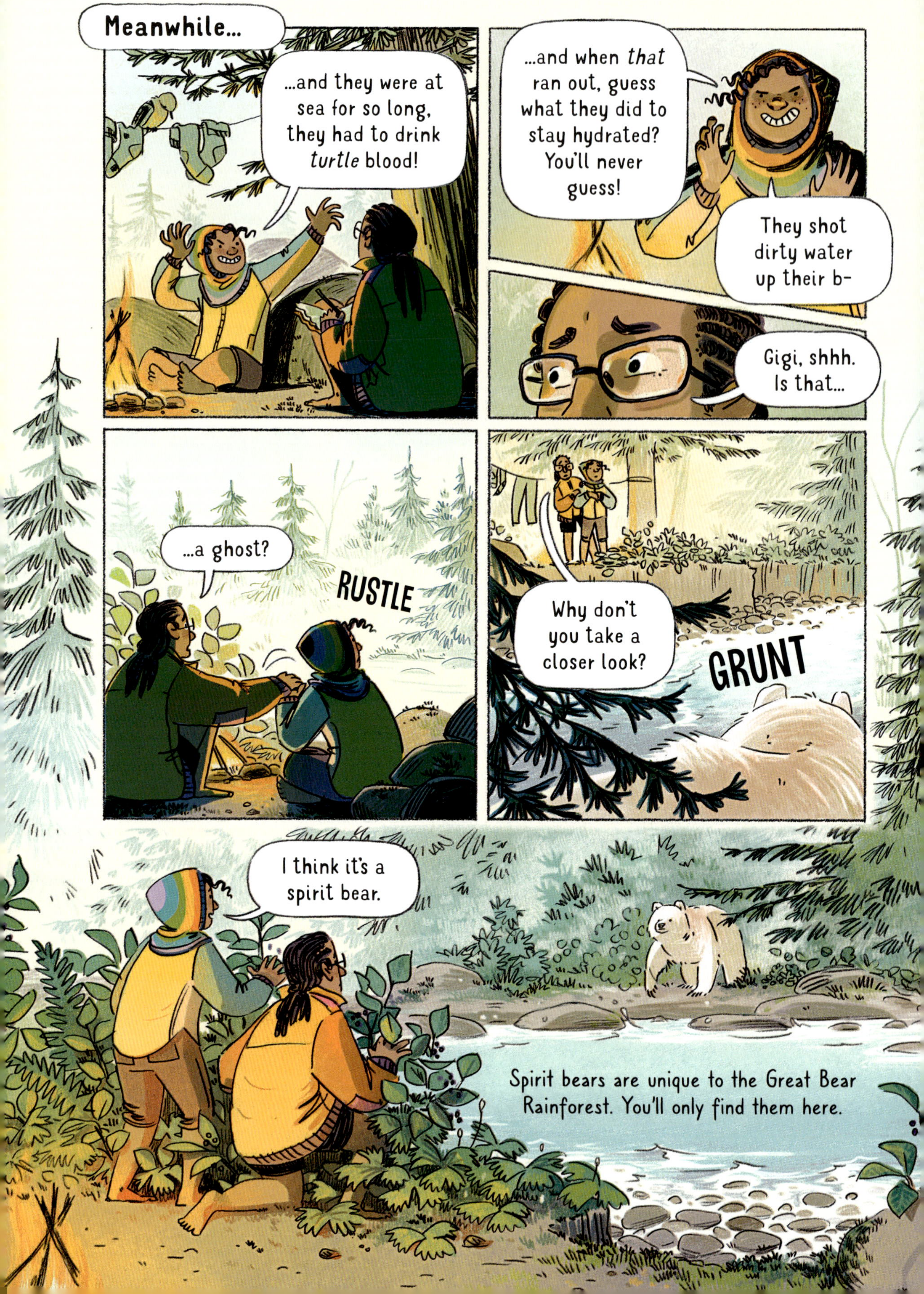
Meanwhile...
...and they were at sea for so long, they had to drink *turtle* blood!
...and when *that* ran out, guess what they did to stay hydrated? You'll never guess!
They shot dirty water up their b-
Gigi, shhh. Is that...
...a ghost?
RUSTLE
Why don't you take a closer look?
GRUNT
I think it's a spirit bear.
Spirit bears are unique to the Great Bear Rainforest. You'll only find them here.

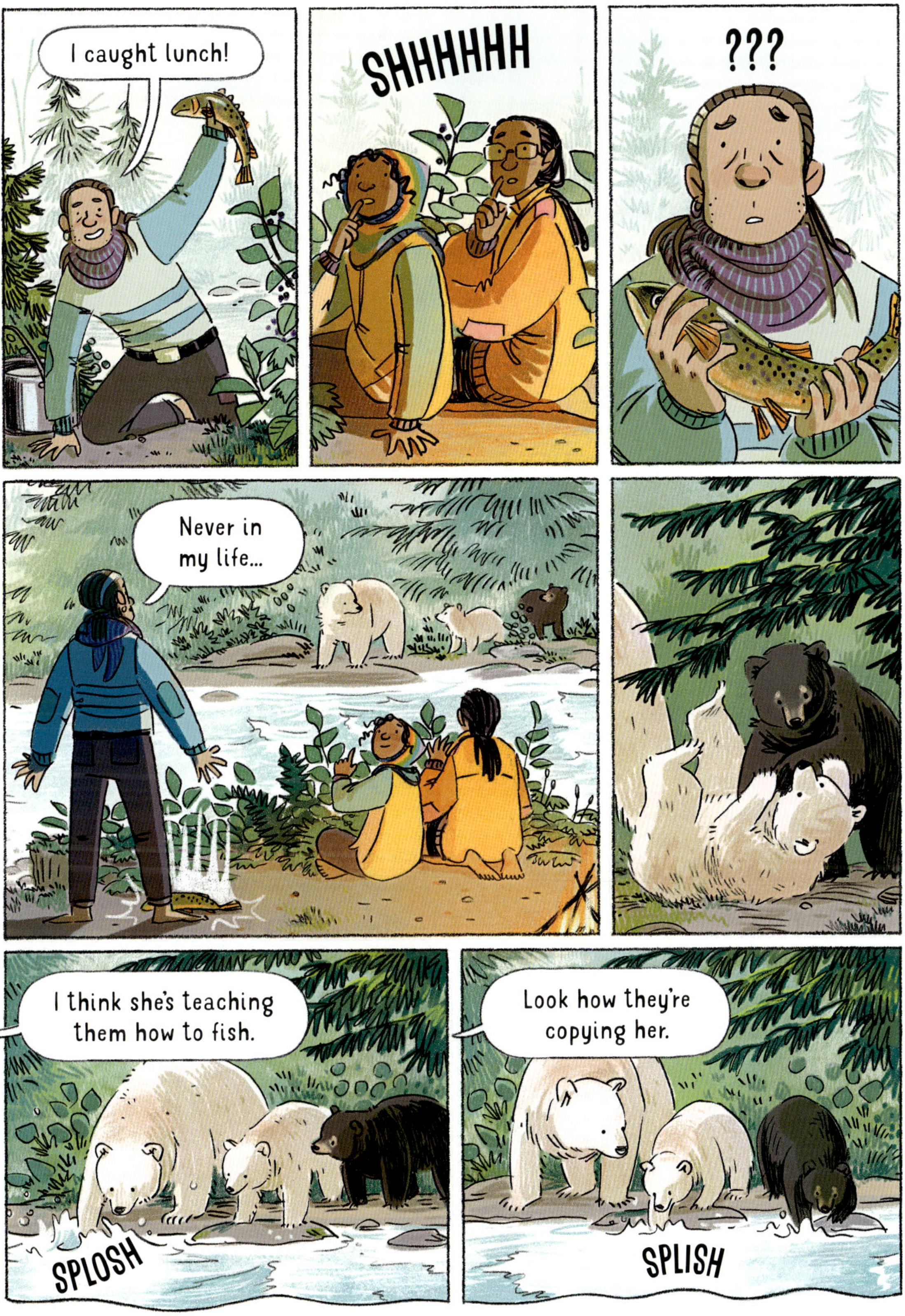
I caught lunch!
SHHHHHH
???
Never in my life...
I think she's teaching them how to fish.
SPLOSH
Look how they're copying her.
SPLISH

A mother bear stays with her cubs until they're about 18 months old. She teaches them all they need to know to survive – and will fight to the death to protect them.

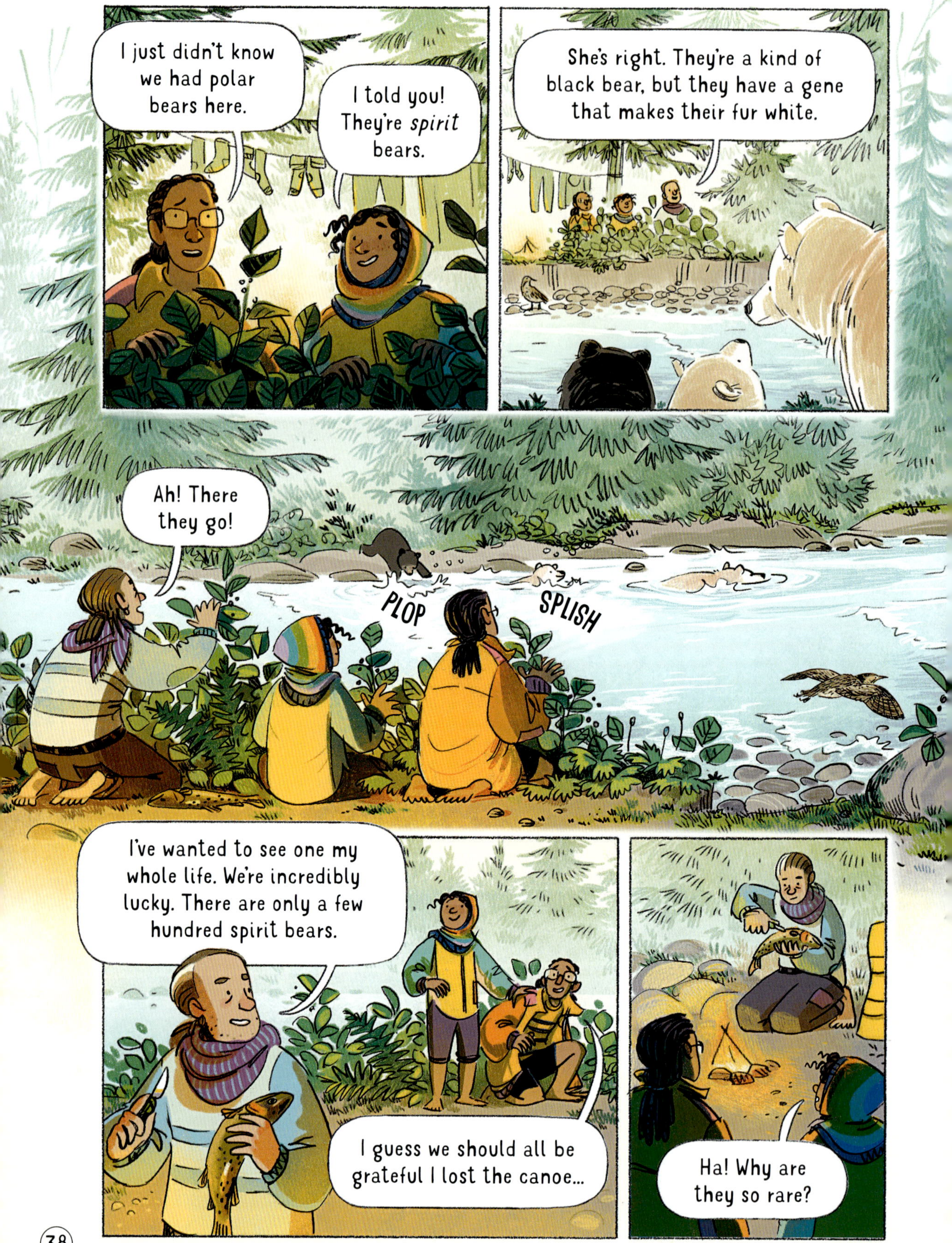
I just didn't know we had polar bears here.
I told you! They're *spirit* bears.
She's right. They're a kind of black bear, but they have a gene that makes their fur white.
Ah! There they go!
PLOP
SPLISH
I've wanted to see one my whole life. We're incredibly lucky. There are only a few hundred spirit bears.
I guess we should all be grateful I lost the canoe...
Ha! Why are they so rare?

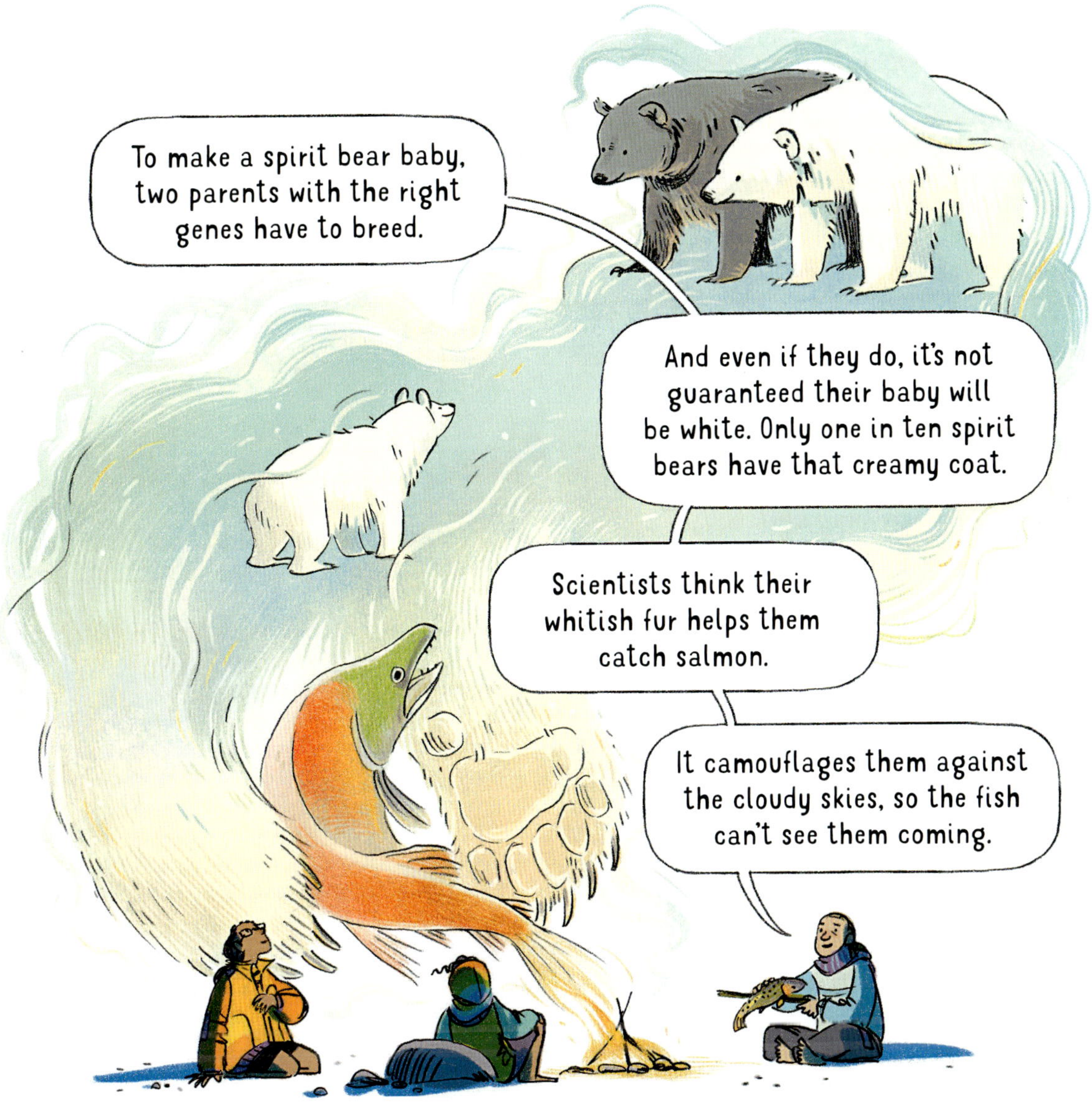
To make a spirit bear baby, two parents with the right genes have to breed.
And even if they do, it's not guaranteed their baby will be white. Only one in ten spirit bears have that creamy coat.
Scientists think their whitish fur helps them catch salmon.
It camouflages them against the cloudy skies, so the fish can't see them coming.

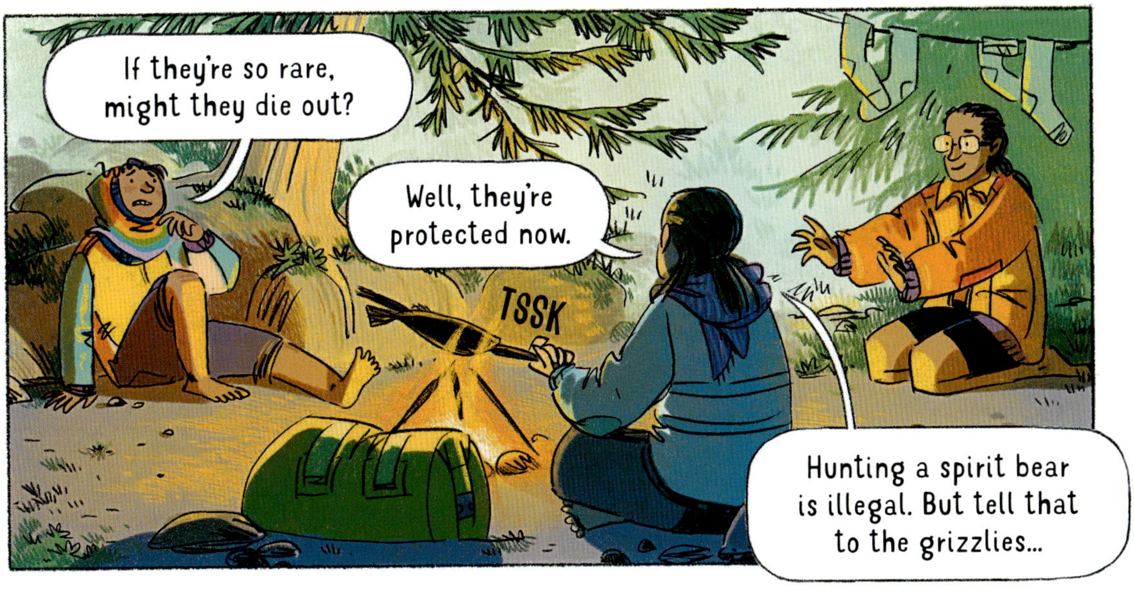
If they're so rare, might they die out?
Well, they're protected now.
TSSK
Hunting a spirit bear is illegal. But tell that to the grizzlies...

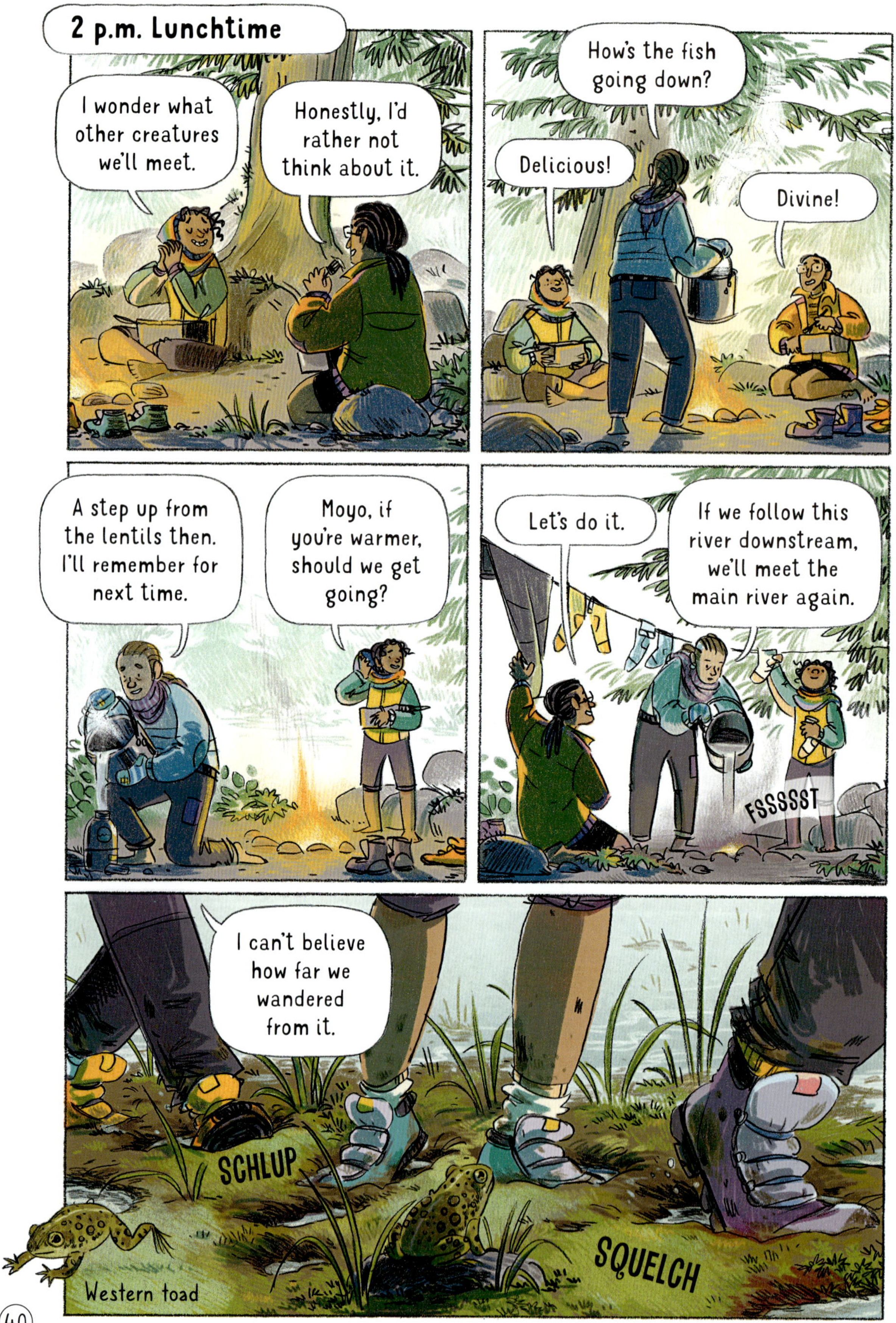

2 p.m. Lunchtime
I wonder what other creatures we'll meet.
Honestly, I'd rather not think about it.
How's the fish going down?
Delicious!
Divine!
A step up from the lentils then. I'll remember for next time.
Moyo, if you're warmer, should we get going?
Let's do it.
If we follow this river downstream, we'll meet the main river again.
FSSSSST
I can't believe how far we wandered from it.
SCHLUP
SQUELCH
Western toad

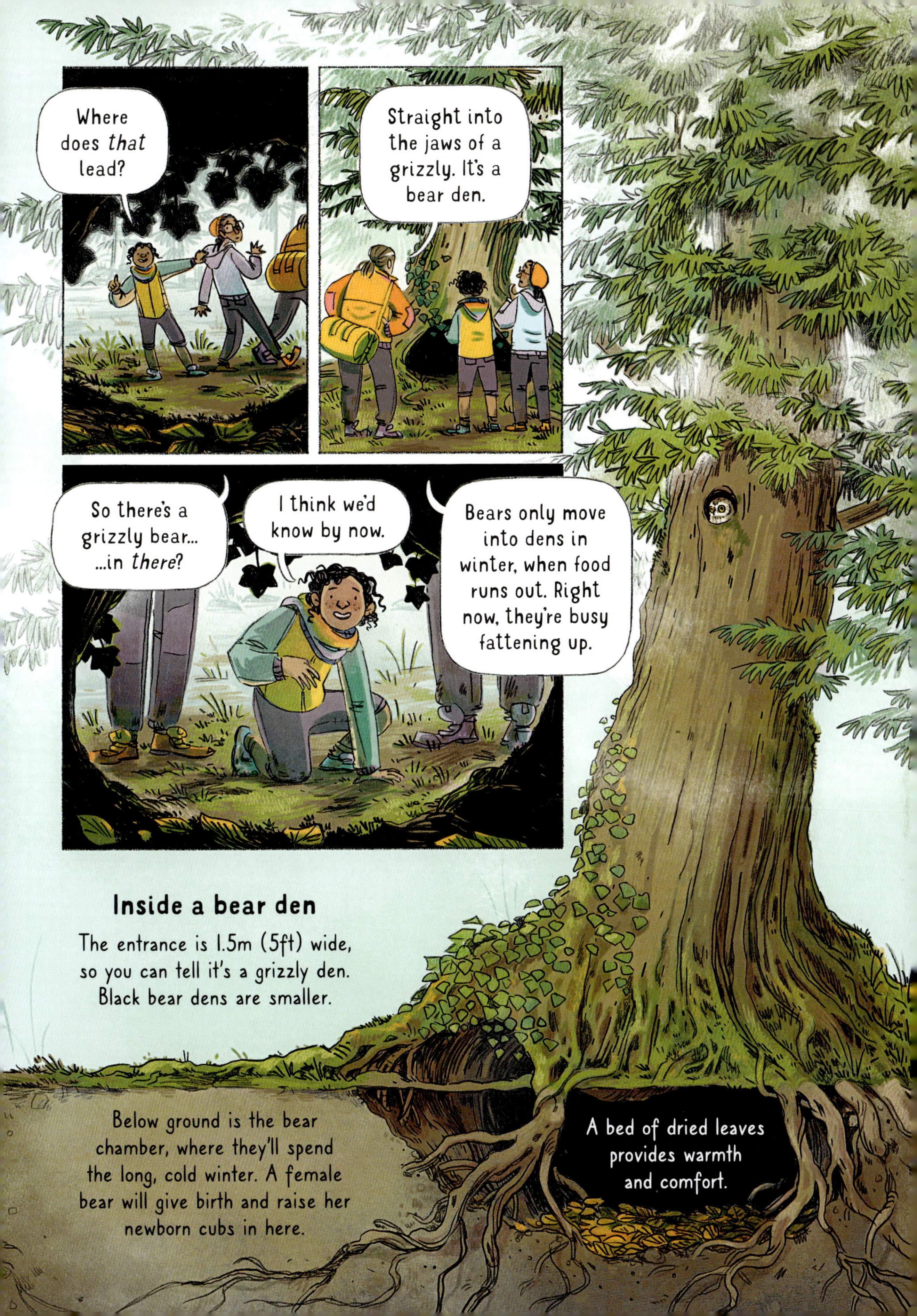

Where does *that* lead?
Straight into the jaws of a grizzly. It's a bear den.
So there's a grizzly bear... ...in *there*?
I think we'd know by now.
Bears only move into dens in winter, when food runs out. Right now, they're busy fattening up.
Inside a bear den
The entrance is 1.5m (5ft) wide, so you can tell it's a grizzly den. Black bear dens are smaller.
Below ground is the bear chamber, where they'll spend the long, cold winter. A female bear will give birth and raise her newborn cubs in here.
A bed of dried leaves provides warmth and comfort.

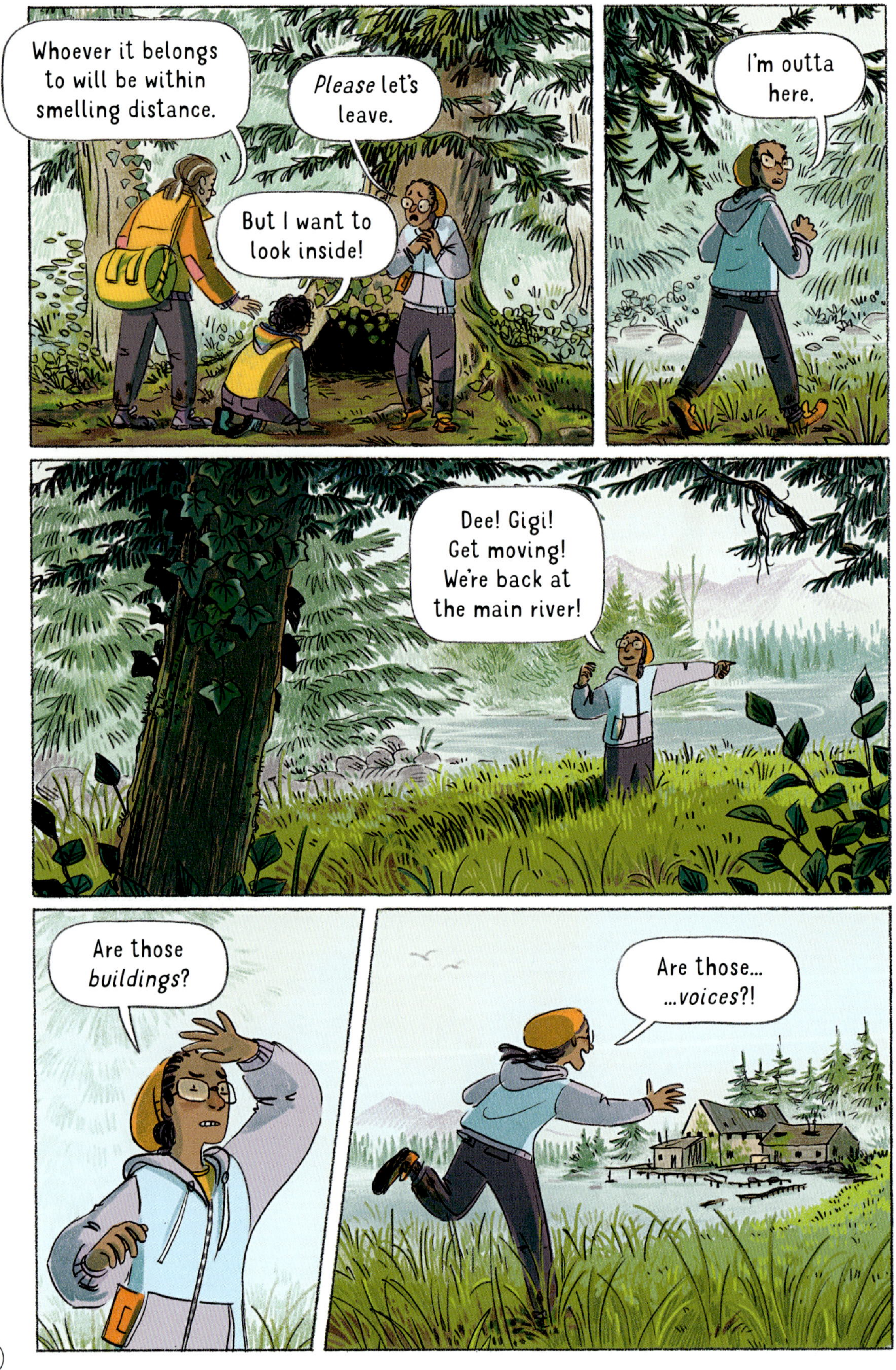
Whoever it belongs to will be within smelling distance.
Please let's leave.
But I want to look inside!
I'm outta here.
Dee! Gigi! Get moving! We're back at the main river!
Are those *buildings*?
Are those... ...*voices*?!

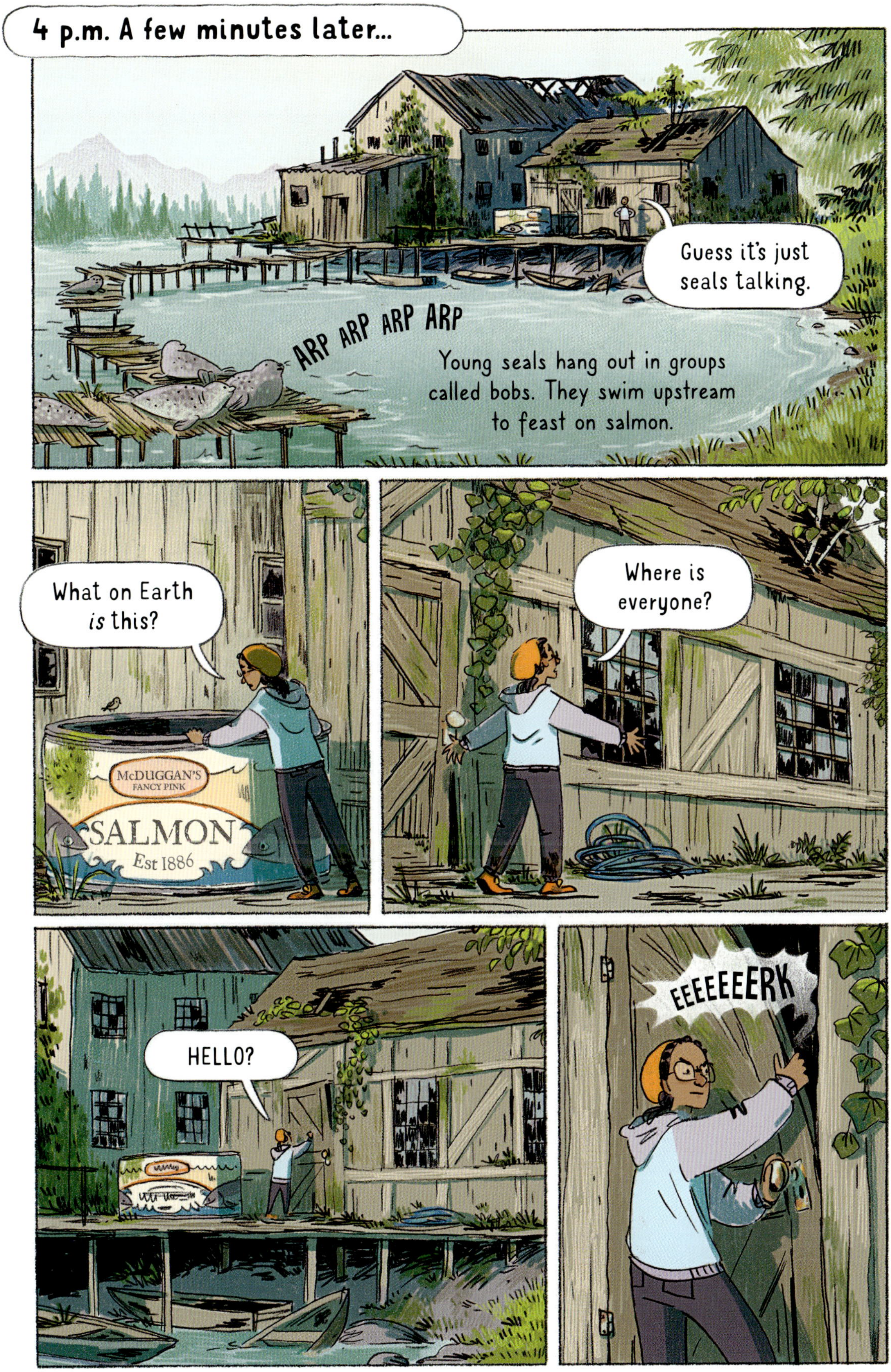
4 p.m. A few minutes later...
Guess it's just seals talking.
ARP ARP ARP ARP
Young seals hang out in groups called bobs. They swim upstream to feast on salmon.
What on Earth *is* this?
McDUGGAN'S
FANCY PINK
SALMON
Est 1886
Where is everyone?
HELLO?
EEEEEEERK

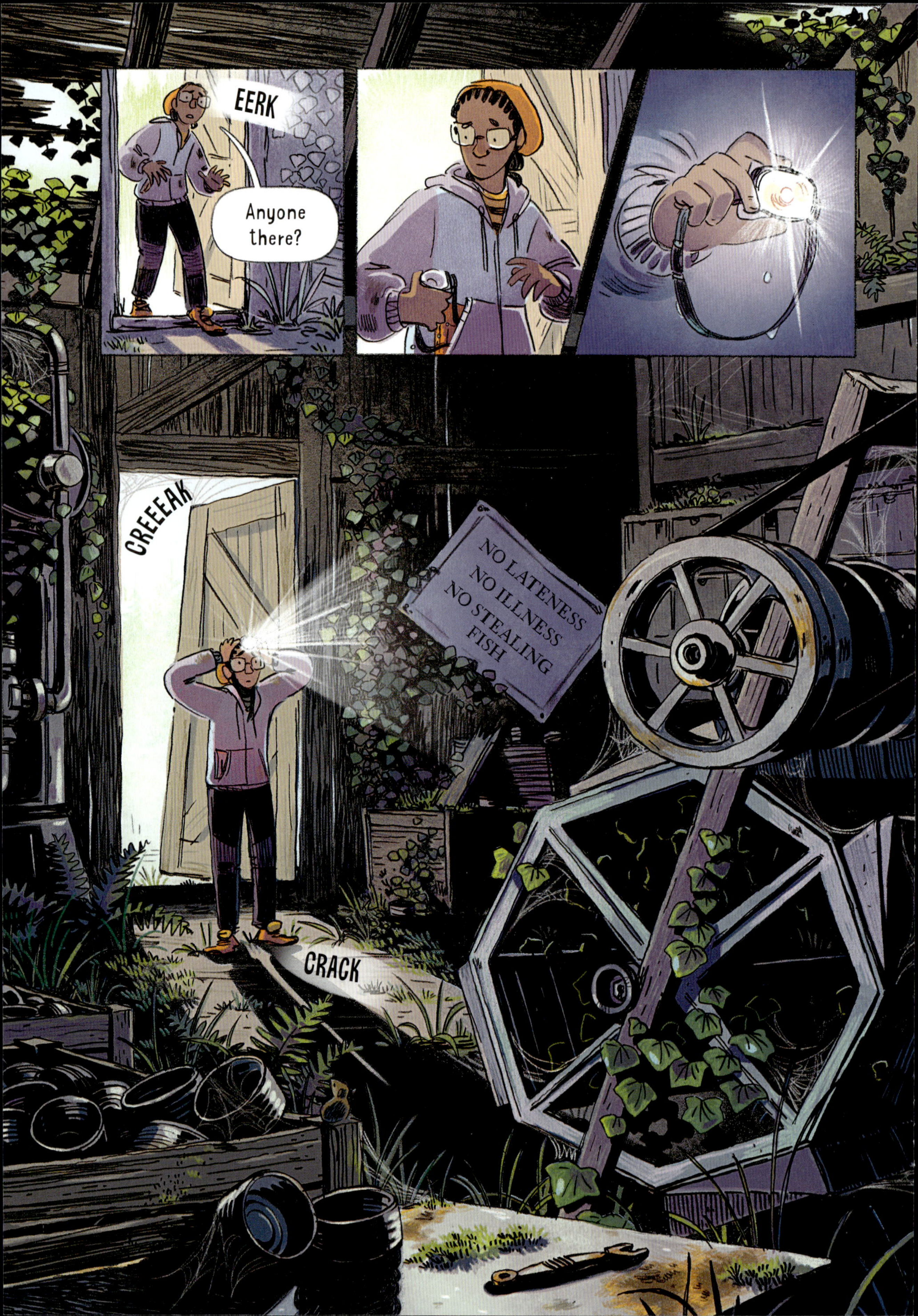
EERK
Anyone there?
CREEEAK
NO LATENESS
NO ILLNESS
NO STEALING
FISH
CRACK

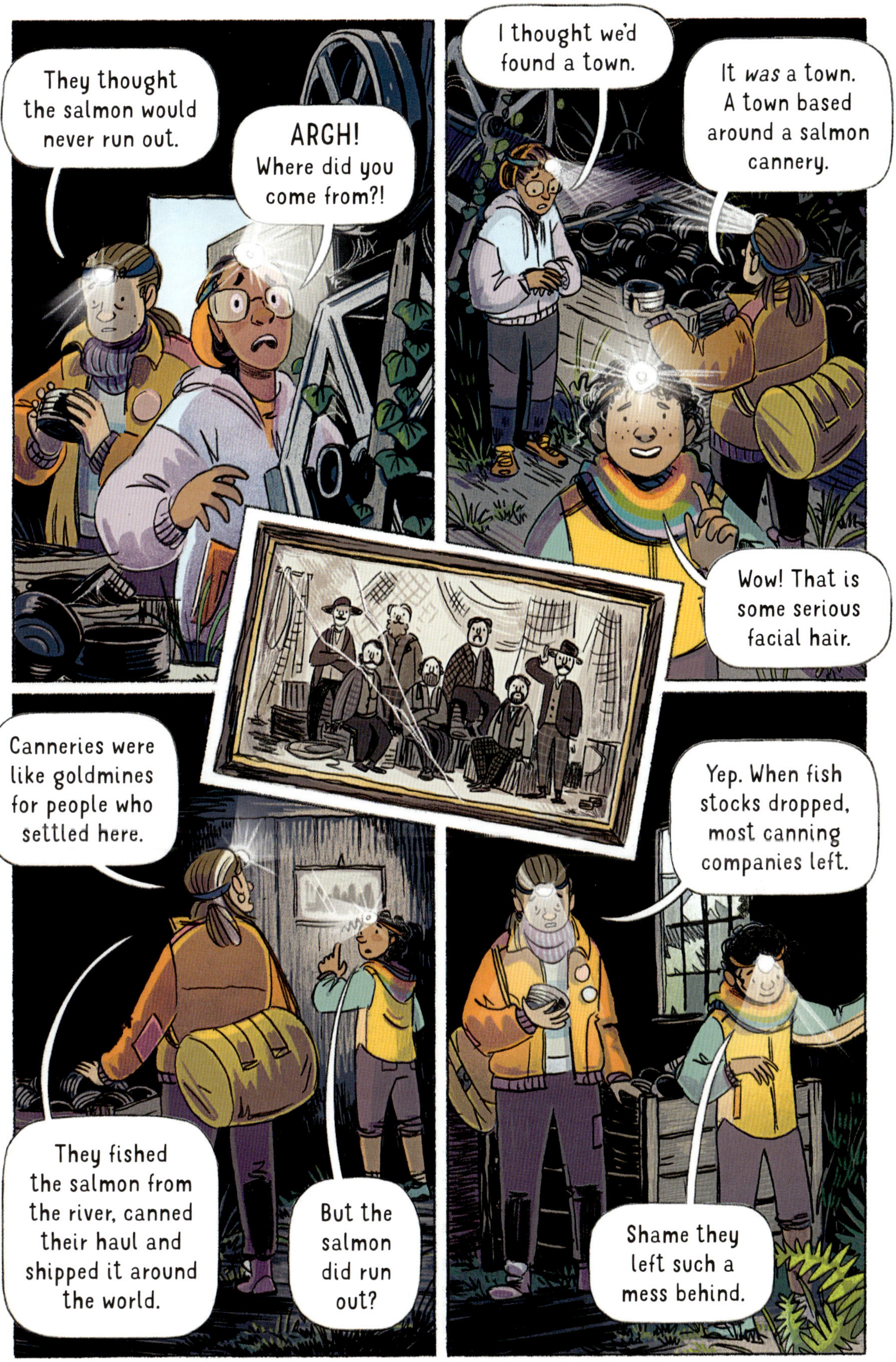
They thought the salmon would never run out.
ARGH! Where did you come from?!
I thought we'd found a town.
It *was* a town. A town based around a salmon cannery.
Wow! That is some serious facial hair.
Canneries were like goldmines for people who settled here.
They fished the salmon from the river, canned their haul and shipped it around the world.
But the salmon did run out?
Yep. When fish stocks dropped, most canning companies left.
Shame they left such a mess behind.

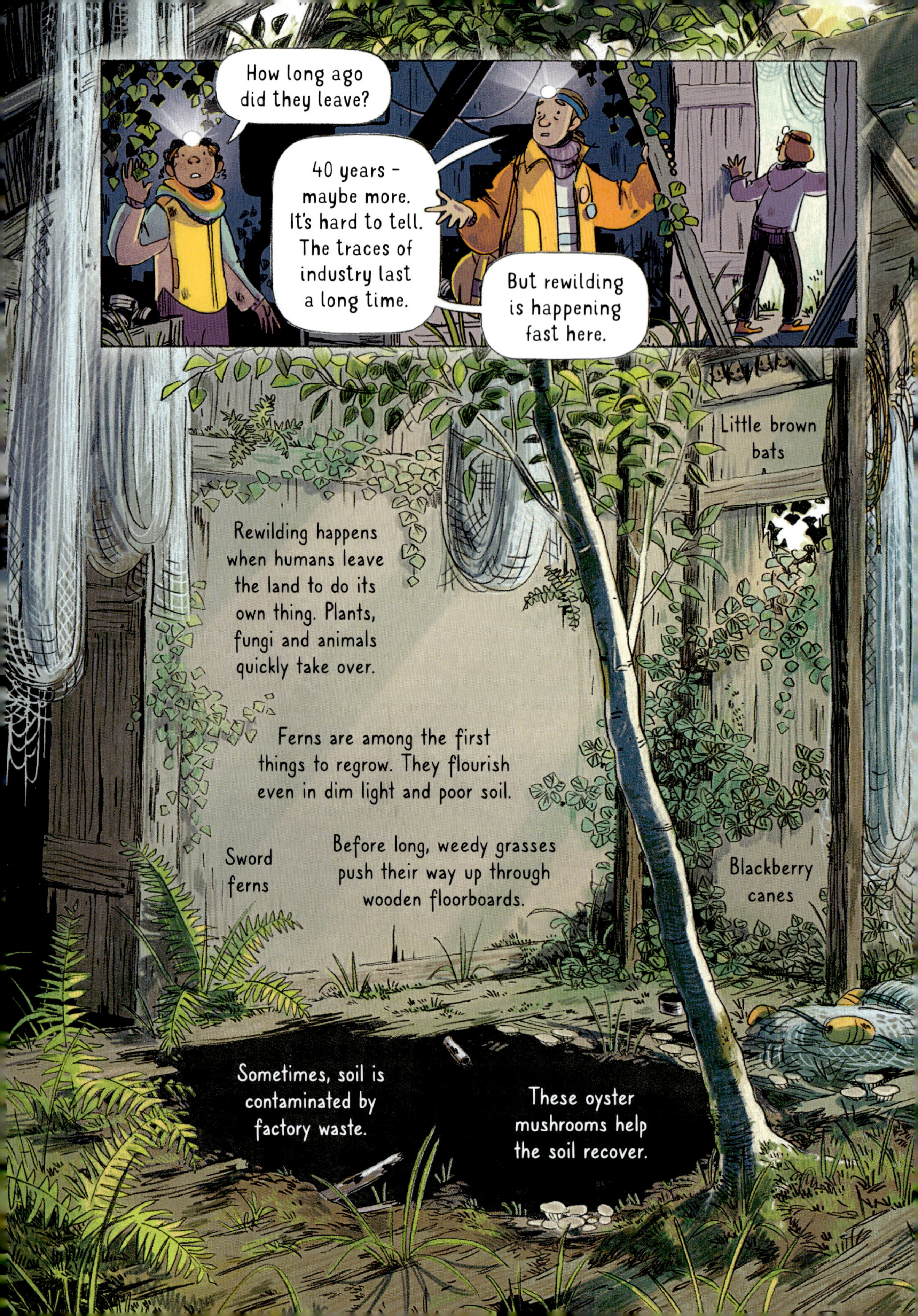

How long ago did they leave?
40 years - maybe more. It's hard to tell. The traces of industry last a long time.
But rewilding is happening fast here.
Little brown bats
Rewilding happens when humans leave the land to do its own thing. Plants, fungi and animals quickly take over.
Ferns are among the first things to regrow. They flourish even in dim light and poor soil.
Sword ferns
Before long, weedy grasses push their way up through wooden floorboards.
Blackberry canes
Sometimes, soil is contaminated by factory waste.
These oyster mushrooms help the soil recover.

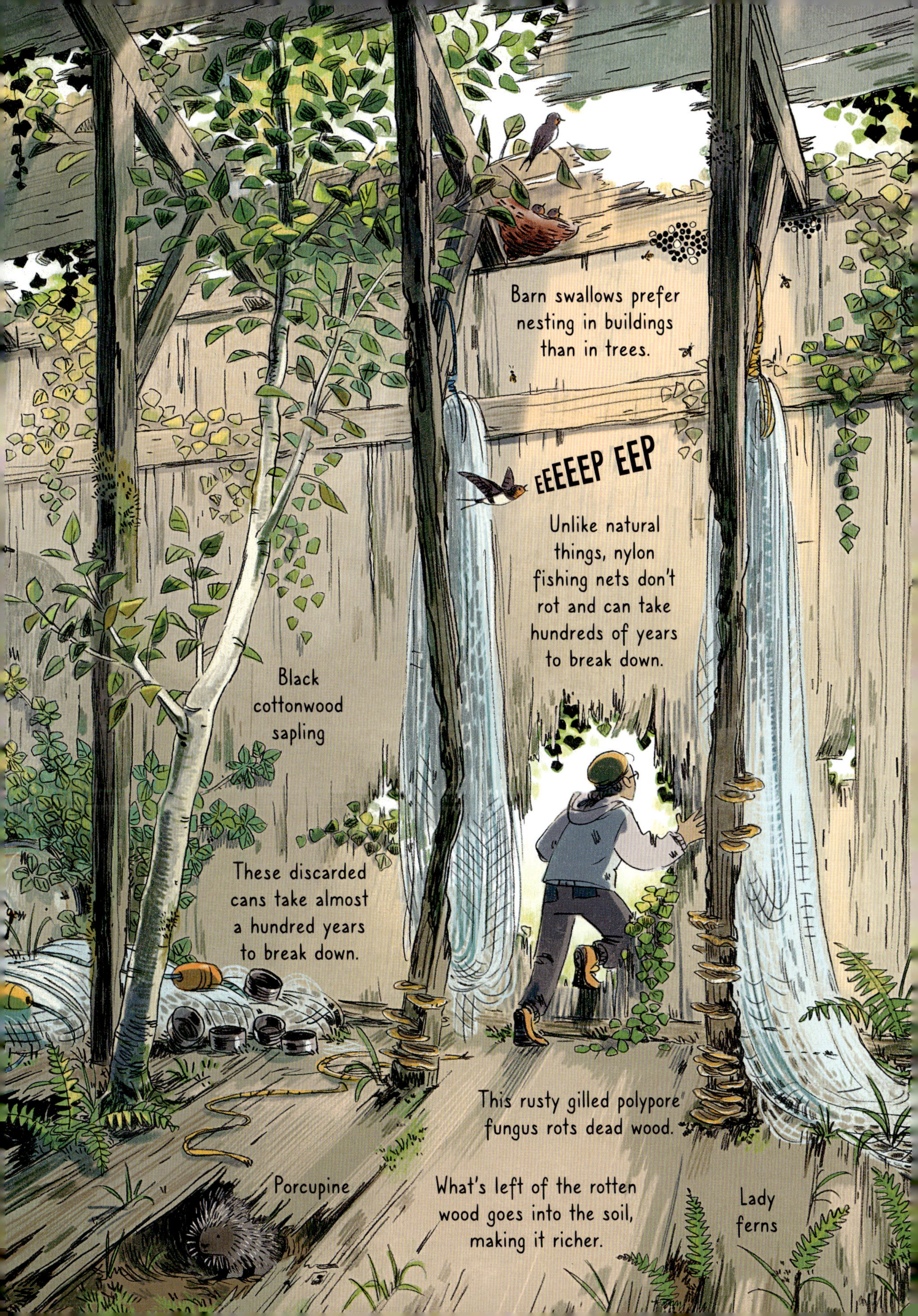
Barn swallows prefer nesting in buildings than in trees.
EEEEEP EEP
Unlike natural things, nylon fishing nets don't rot and can take hundreds of years to break down.
Black cottonwood sapling
These discarded cans take almost a hundred years to break down.
This rusty gilled polypore fungus rots dead wood.
Porcupine
What's left of the rotten wood goes into the soil, making it richer.
Lady ferns

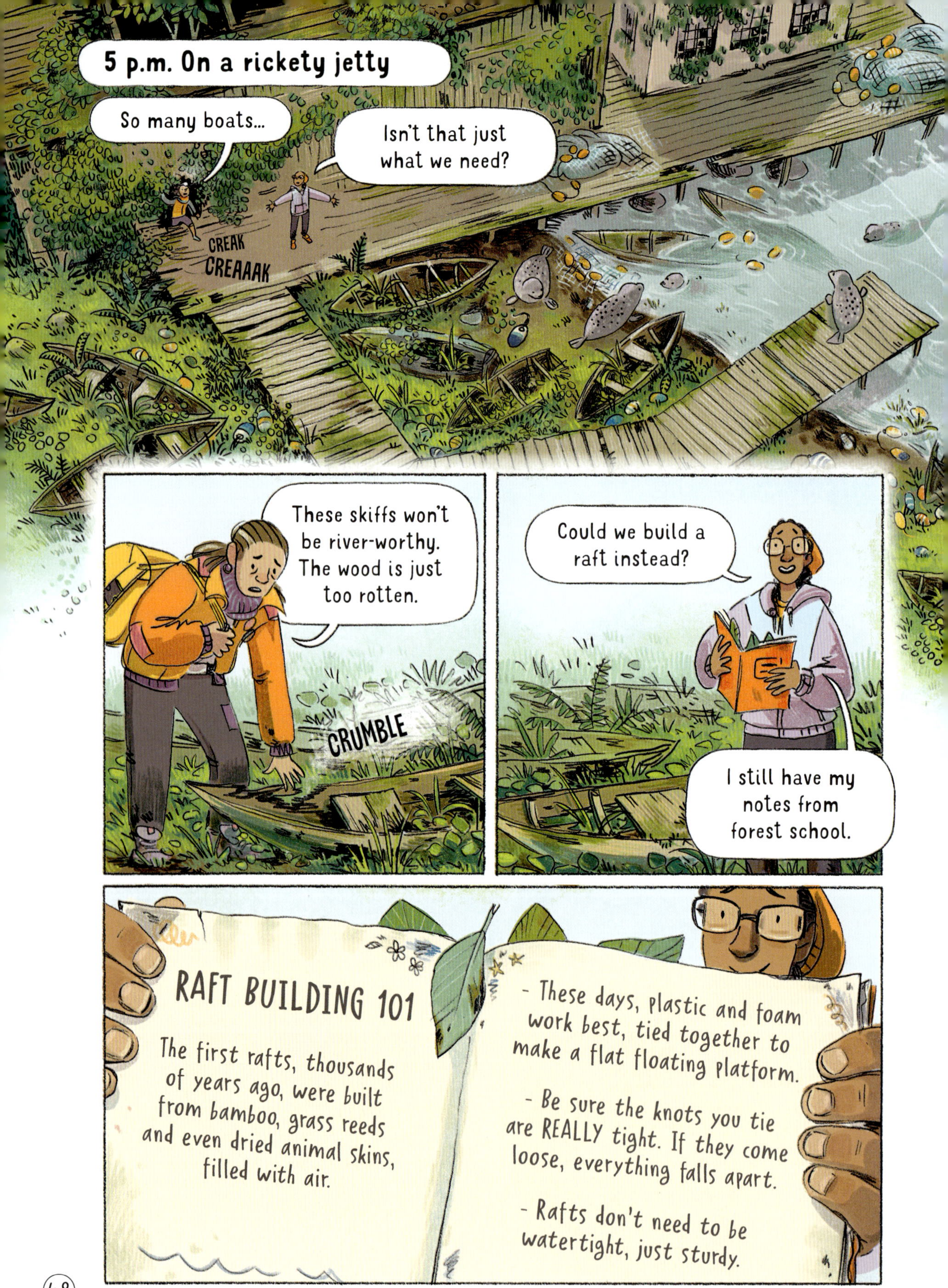
5 p.m. On a rickety jetty
So many boats...
Isn't that just what we need?
CREAK
CREAAAK
These skiffs won't be river-worthy. The wood is just too rotten.
CRUMBLE
Could we build a raft instead?
I still have my notes from forest school.
RAFT BUILDING 101
The first rafts, thousands of years ago, were built from bamboo, grass reeds and even dried animal skins, filled with air.
- These days, plastic and foam work best, tied together to make a flat floating platform.
- Be sure the knots you tie are REALLY tight. If they come loose, everything falls apart.
- Rafts don't need to be watertight, just sturdy.

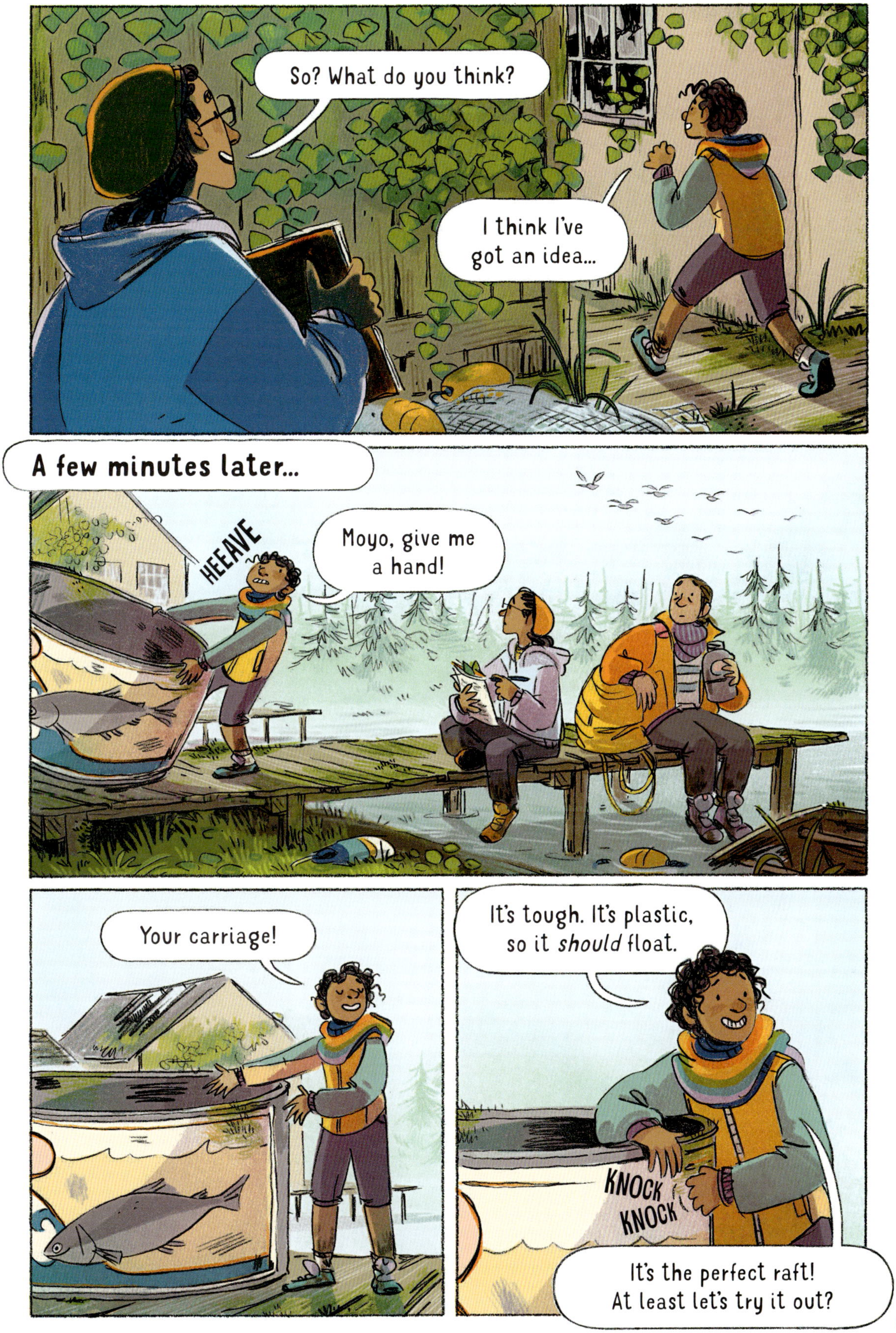
So? What do you think?
I think I've got an idea...
A few minutes later...
HEEAVE
Moyo, give me a hand!
Your carriage!
It's tough. It's plastic, so it *should* float.
KNOCK KNOCK
It's the perfect raft! At least let's try it out?

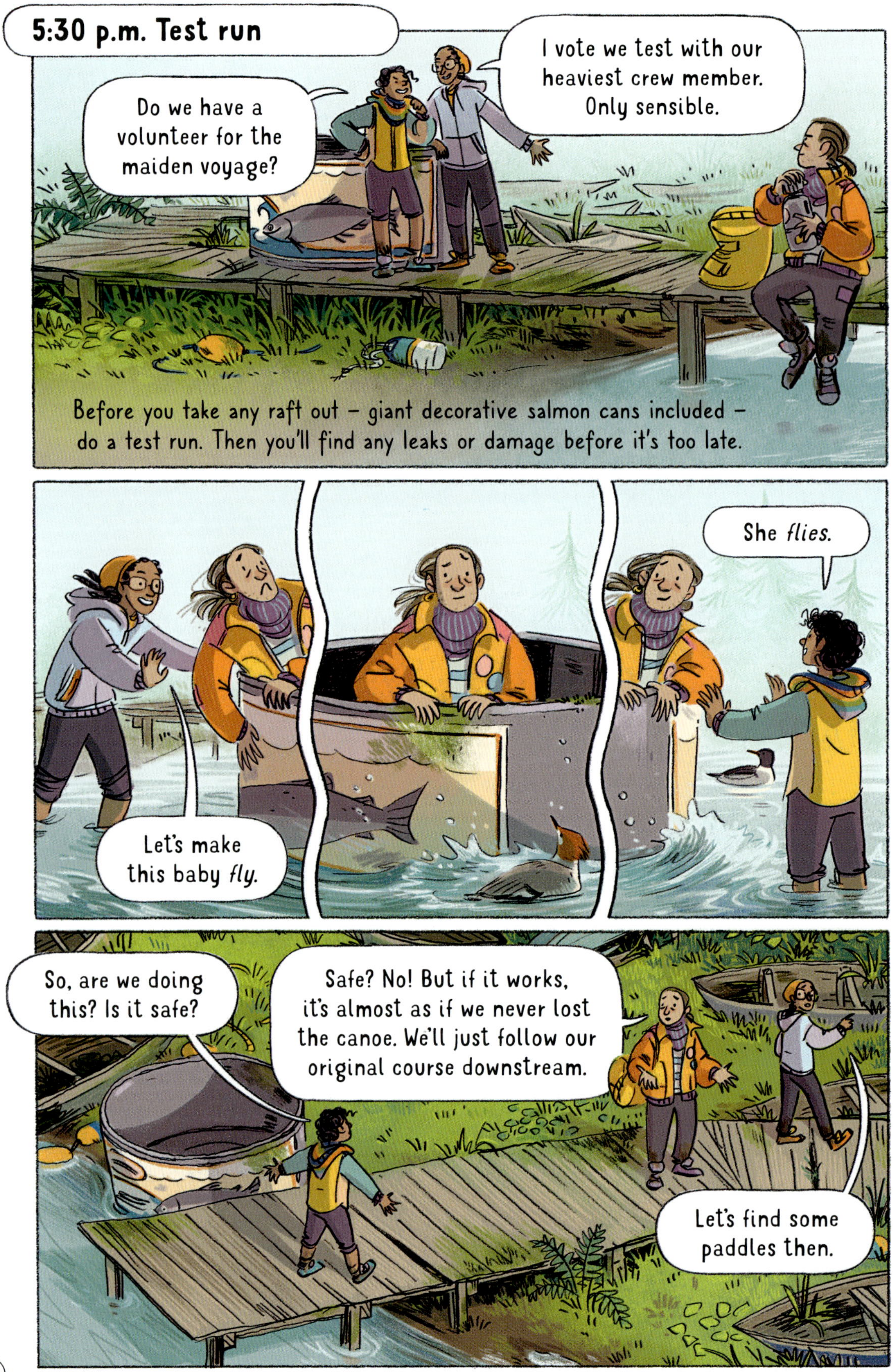
5:30 p.m. Test run
Do we have a volunteer for the maiden voyage?
I vote we test with our heaviest crew member. Only sensible.
Before you take any raft out – giant decorative salmon cans included – do a test run. Then you'll find any leaks or damage before it's too late.
Let's make this baby *fly*.
She *flies*.
So, are we doing this? Is it safe?
Safe? No! But if it works, it's almost as if we never lost the canoe. We'll just follow our original course downstream.
Let's find some paddles then.

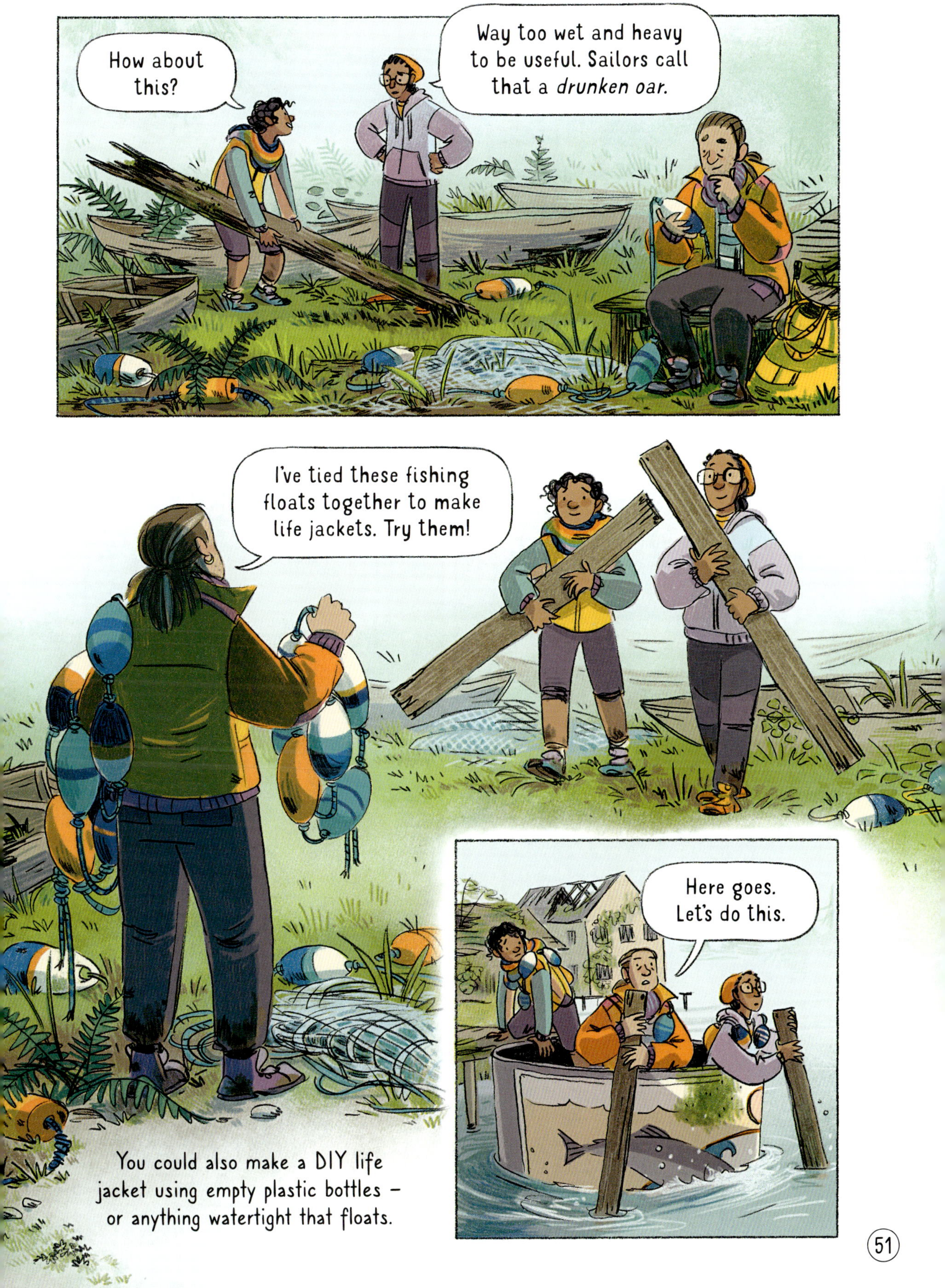
How about this?
Way too wet and heavy to be useful. Sailors call that a *drunken oar.*
I've tied these fishing floats together to make life jackets. Try them!
You could also make a DIY life jacket using empty plastic bottles – or anything watertight that floats.
Here goes. Let's do this.

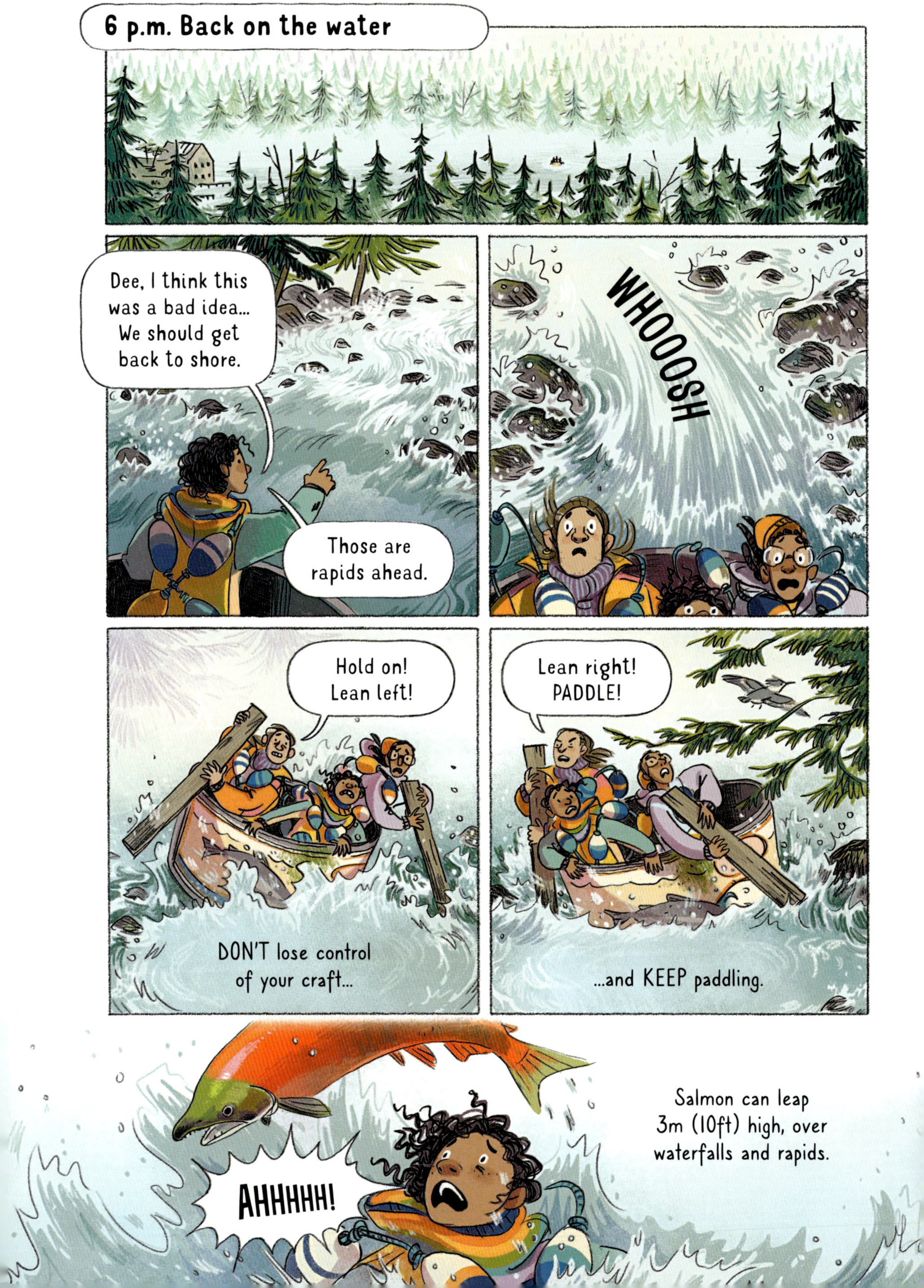
6 p.m. Back on the water
Dee, I think this was a bad idea... We should get back to shore.
Those are rapids ahead.
WHOOOSH
Hold on! Lean left!
DON'T lose control of your craft...
Lean right! PADDLE!
...and KEEP paddling.
AHHHHH!
Salmon can leap 3m (10ft) high, over waterfalls and rapids.

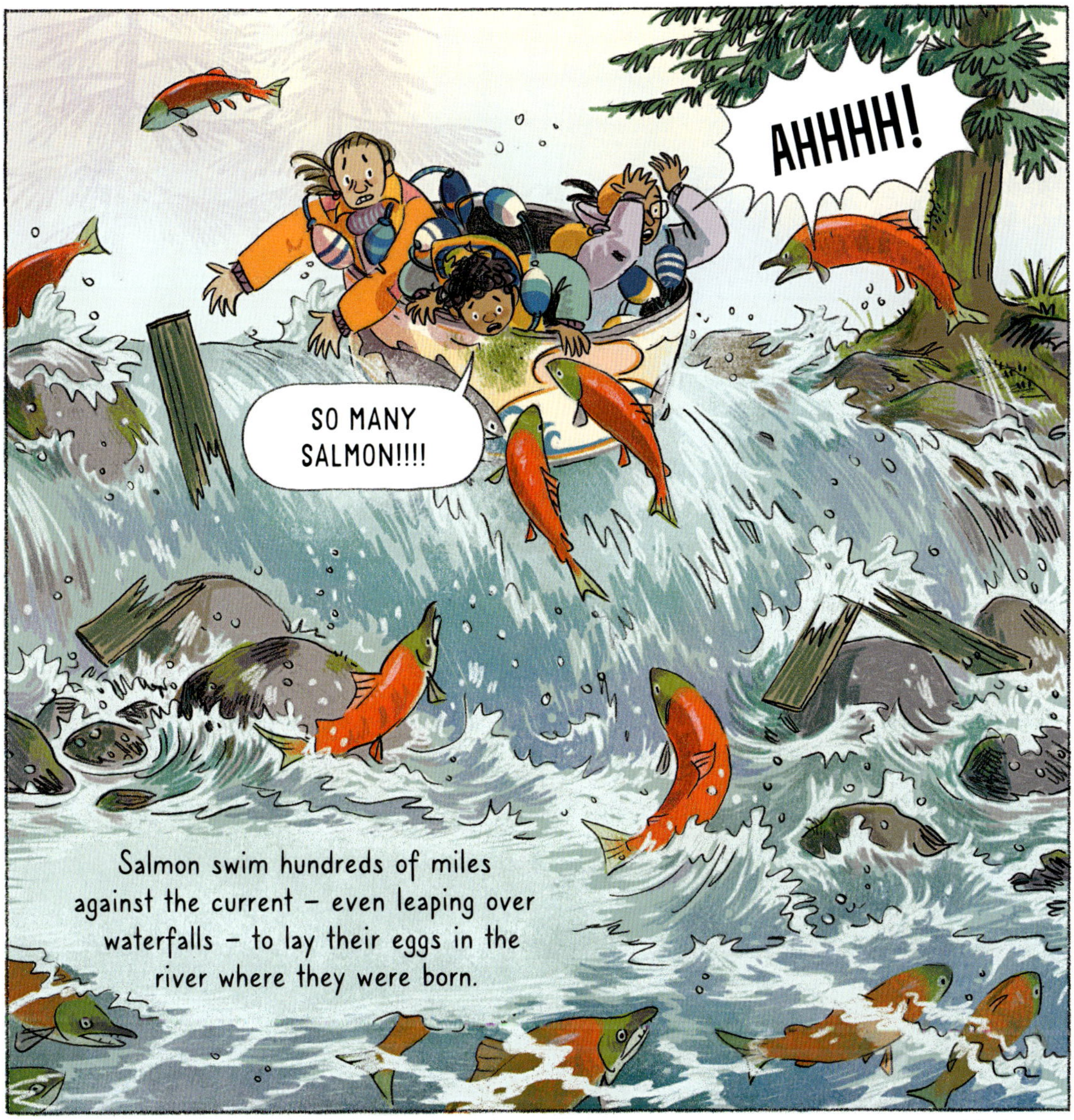
AHHHH!
SO MANY SALMON!!!!
Salmon swim hundreds of miles against the current – even leaping over waterfalls – to lay their eggs in the river where they were born.

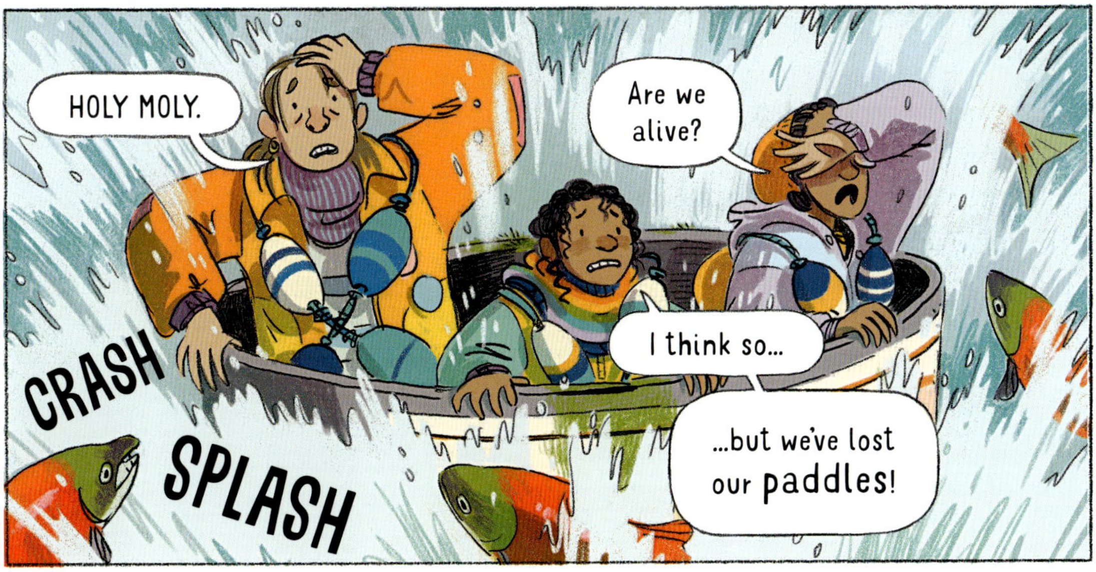
HOLY MOLY.
Are we alive?
I think so...
...but we've lost our paddles!
CRASH
SPLASH

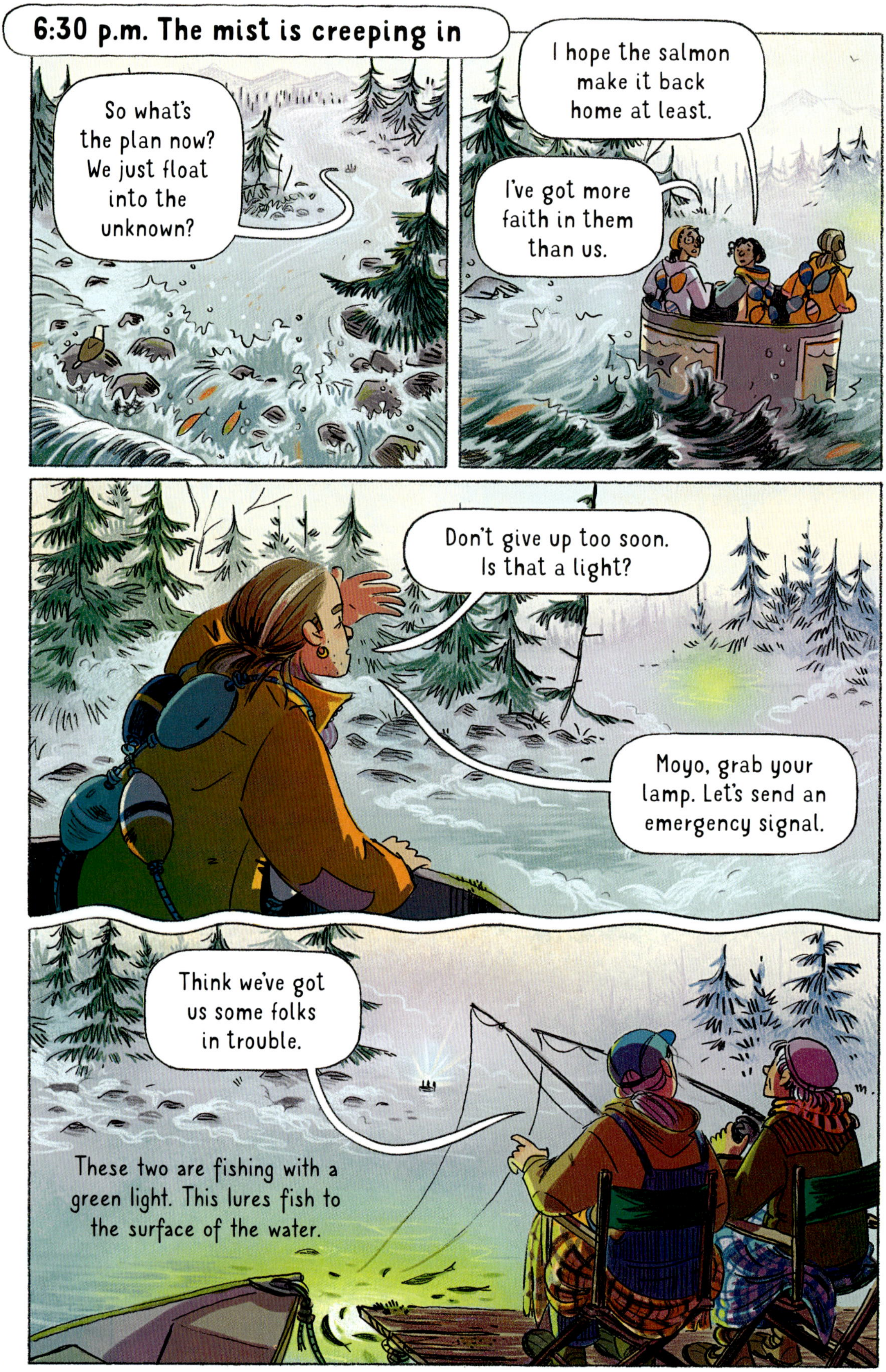
6:30 p.m. The mist is creeping in
So what's the plan now? We just float into the unknown?
I hope the salmon make it back home at least.
I've got more faith in them than us.
Don't give up too soon. Is that a light?
Moyo, grab your lamp. Let's send an emergency signal.
Think we've got us some folks in trouble.
These two are fishing with a green light. This lures fish to the surface of the water.

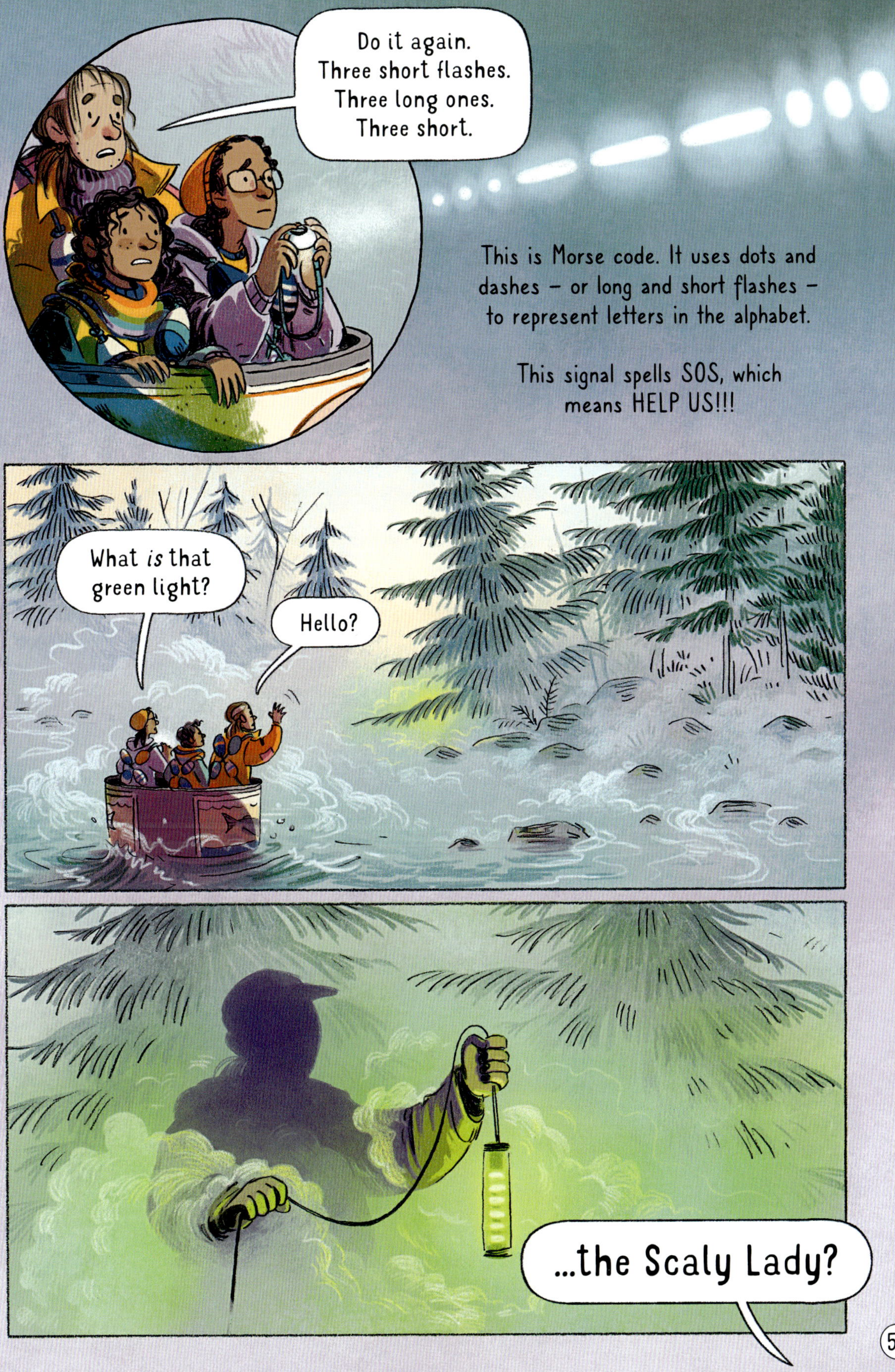

Do it again.
Three short flashes.
Three long ones.
Three short.
This is Morse code. It uses dots and dashes – or long and short flashes – to represent letters in the alphabet.
This signal spells SOS, which means HELP US!!!
What *is* that green light?
Hello?
...the Scaly Lady?

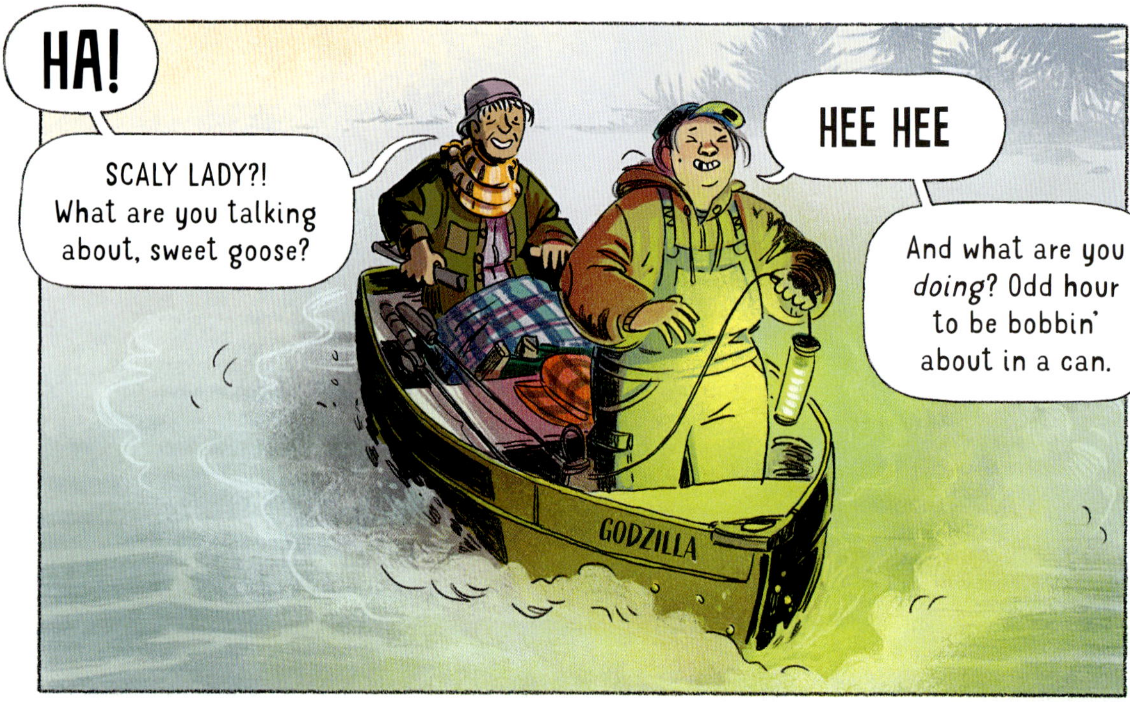
HA!
SCALY LADY?! What are you talking about, sweet goose?
HEE HEE
And what are you *doing*? Odd hour to be bobbin' about in a can.
GODZILLA

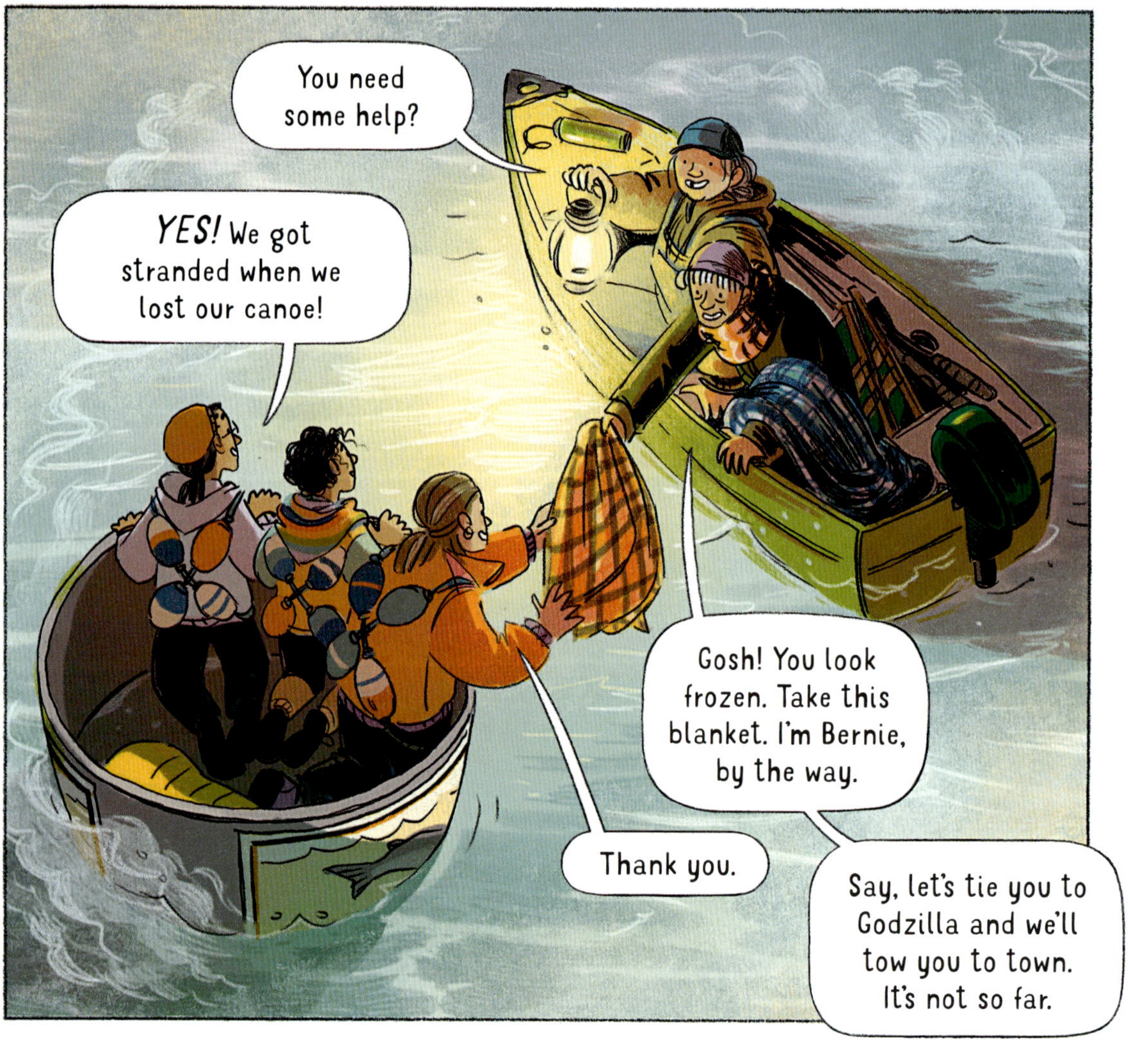
You need some help?
YES! We got stranded when we lost our canoe!
Gosh! You look frozen. Take this blanket. I'm Bernie, by the way.
Thank you.
Say, let's tie you to Godzilla and we'll tow you to town. It's not so far.

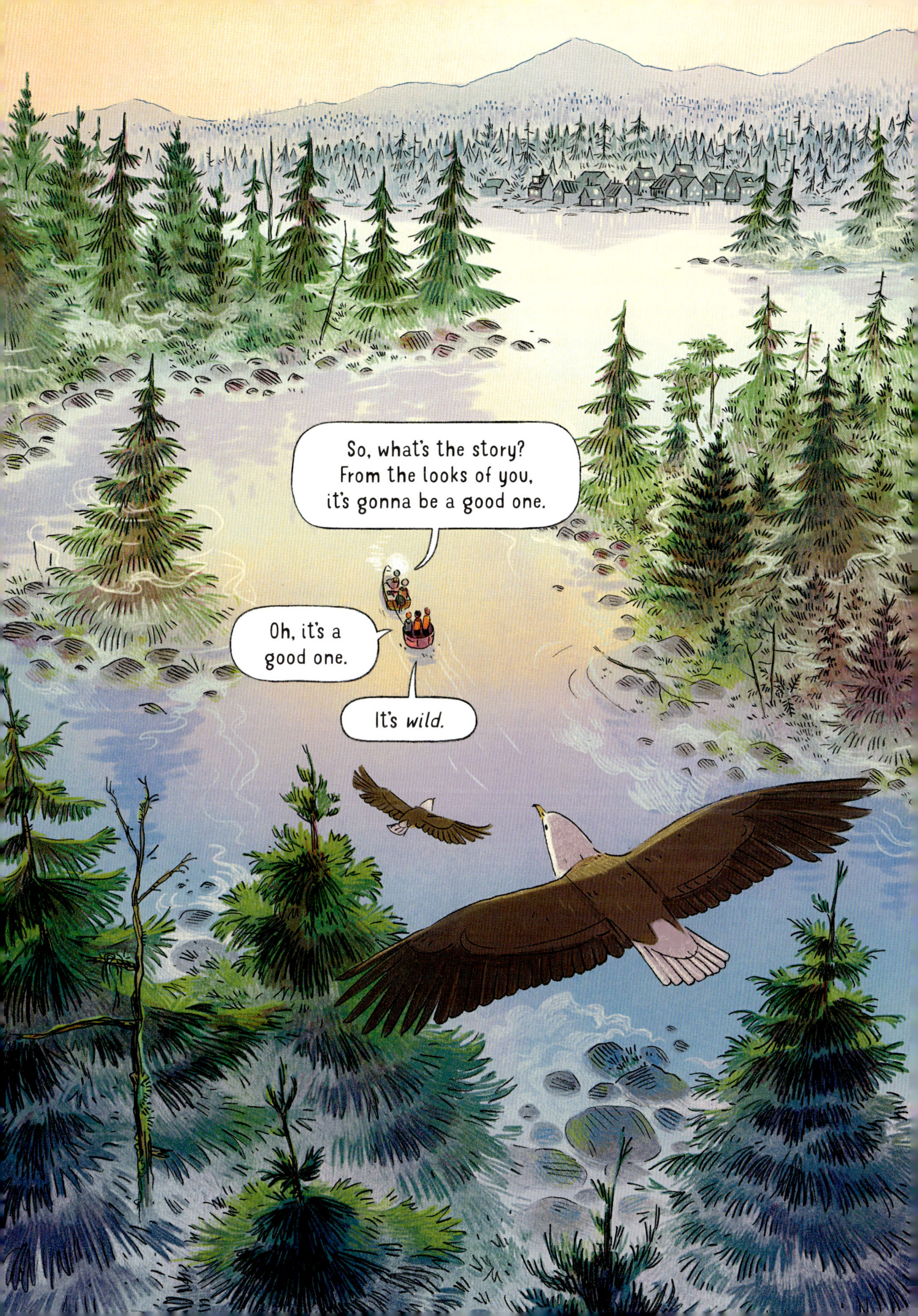
So, what's the story? From the looks of you, it's gonna be a good one.
Oh, it's a good one.
It's *wild.*

So, where's our next wilderness adventure?

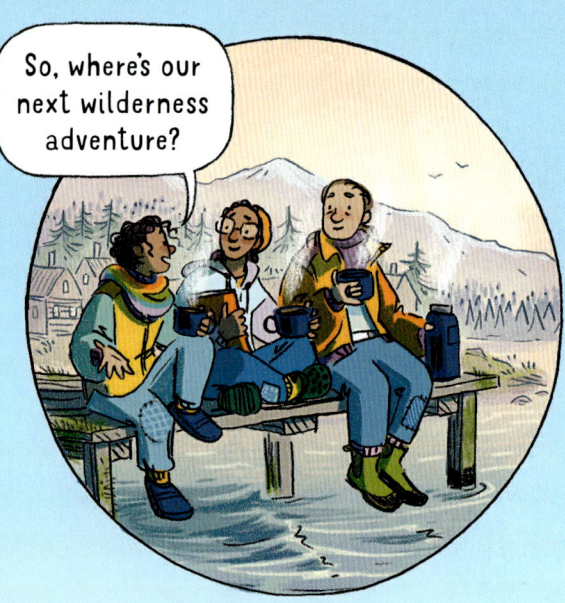

The world's wild places

There's almost nowhere on Earth humans haven't been. People have lived in some of the world's wildest places for thousands of years, protecting the land and caring for the wildlife that makes these areas unique.

Barren salt flats

Bolivia, South America

This vast desert of salt was formed thousands of years ago, when a prehistoric lake dried up. Giant cacti are among the only things to survive, sometimes growing taller than buildings. And you really *don't* want to eat them...

The "Empty Quarter"

Arabian Desert, the Middle East

Imagine sand as far as you can see – and almost nothing else. Some communities roam the desert and a few towns lie at its edge, but with so little water, survival is hard. Days are face-meltingly hot, and nights are bitterly cold.

A vast rainforest

Salonga National Park, Congo Basin

Africa's biggest tropical rainforest is home to many protected species, including forest elephants and pygmy chimpanzees. It's so remote, you can only reach it by boat.

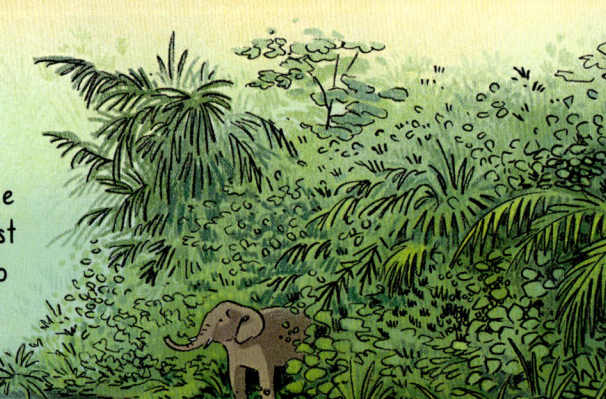

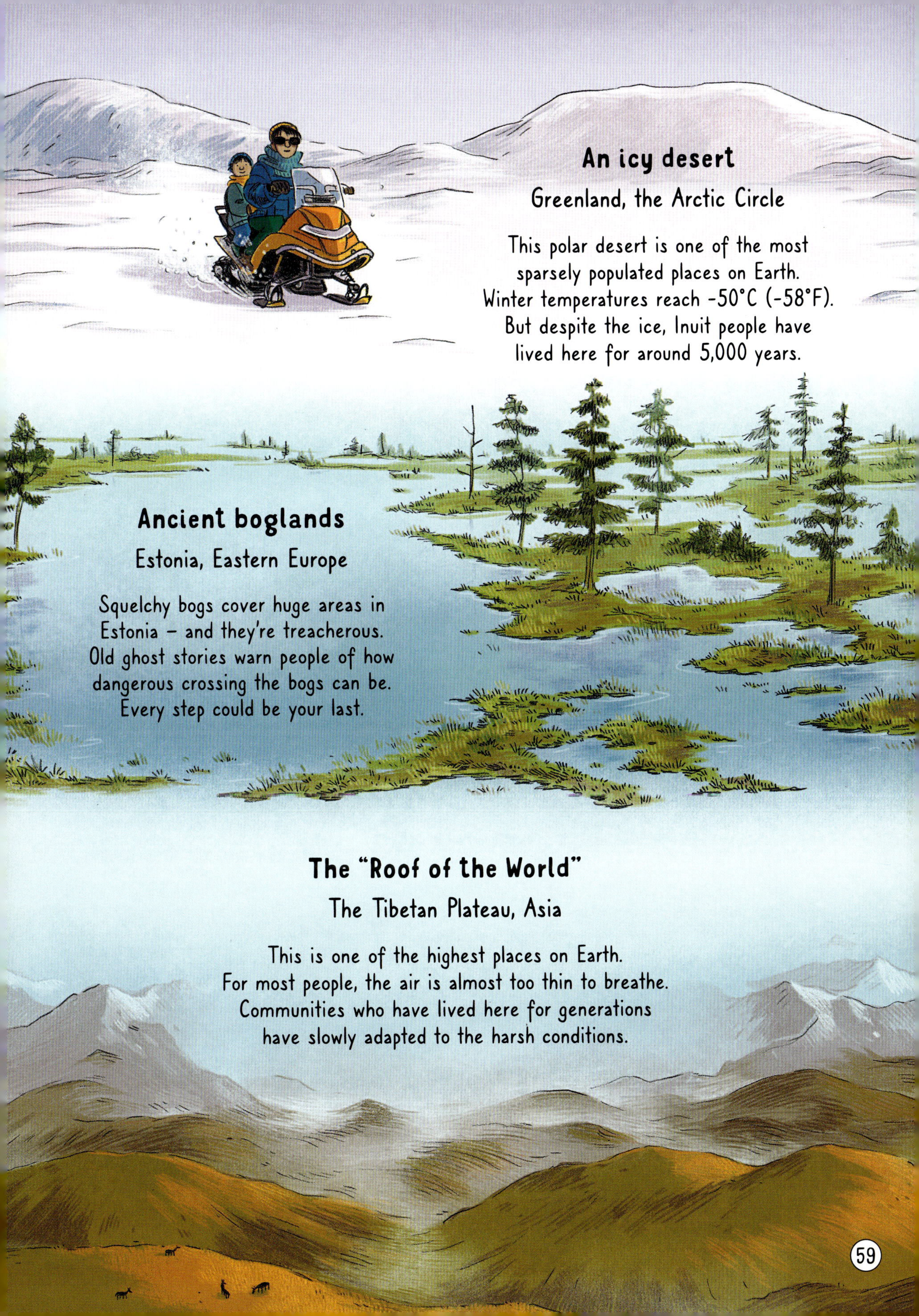

An icy desert

Greenland, the Arctic Circle

This polar desert is one of the most sparsely populated places on Earth. Winter temperatures reach -50°C (-58°F). But despite the ice, Inuit people have lived here for around 5,000 years.

Ancient boglands

Estonia, Eastern Europe

Squelchy bogs cover huge areas in Estonia – and they're treacherous. Old ghost stories warn people of how dangerous crossing the bogs can be. Every step could be your last.

The "Roof of the World"

The Tibetan Plateau, Asia

This is one of the highest places on Earth. For most people, the air is almost too thin to breathe. Communities who have lived here for generations have slowly adapted to the harsh conditions.

Preparing for a wilderness adventure

How to get ready and keep yourself safe.

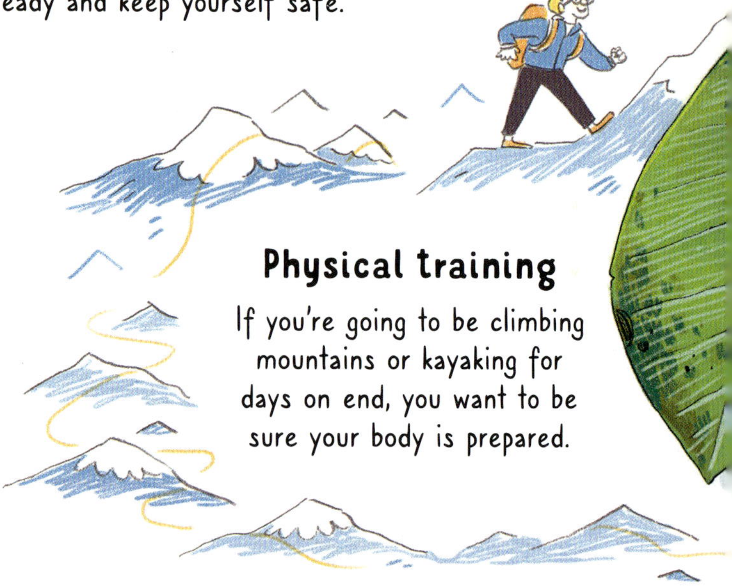

Get permission

Many wilderness areas are home to Indigenous communities who have looked after the land for countless generations. Check it's ok to visit, and be sure to treat sacred land with respect.

Physical training

If you're going to be climbing mountains or kayaking for days on end, you want to be sure your body is prepared.

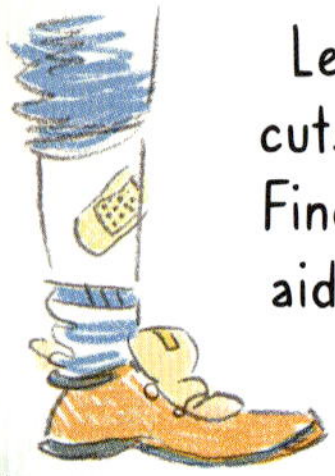

Take a first aid course

Learn what to do in case of cuts, sprains, breaks and bites. Find out what to fill your first aid kit with on the next page.

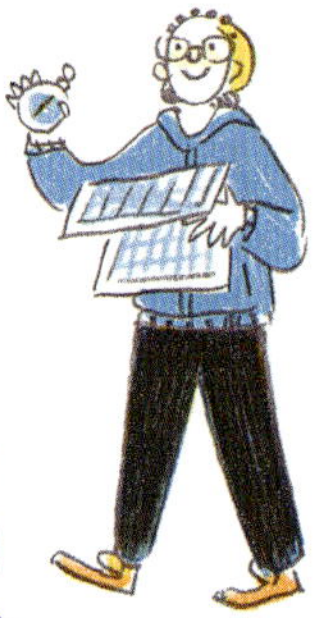

Learn to use a map and compass

Knowing how to read a map is one of the most important wilderness skills you need. You can learn this at home.

Check the weather

In wild places, the weather can change really fast. Never head out in a storm – but always be prepared for one. Check sunrise and sunset times, too.

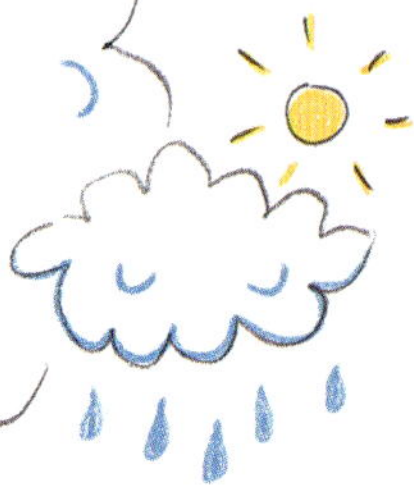

Tell someone where you're going

Let them know when you're due back too. If something goes wrong, they'll know when to call for help. And make sure *you* know the number of local emergency services.

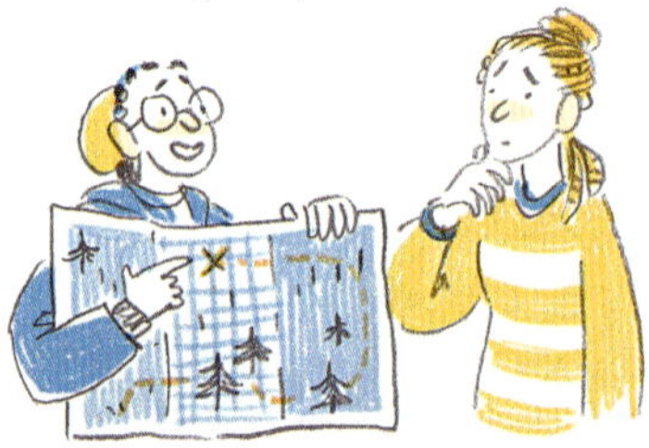

Research the area

Is it mountainous? Boggy? What animals live here? Talk to someone who's been there – and think about finding a local guide. Read a map of the area to get familiar with the lay of the land.

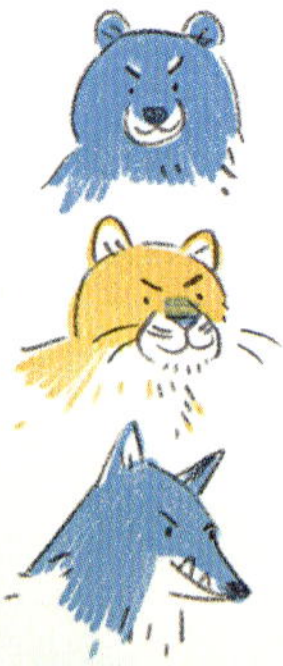

Wilderness essentials

Here's a checklist of things to pack.
Make sure you test it all before you go.

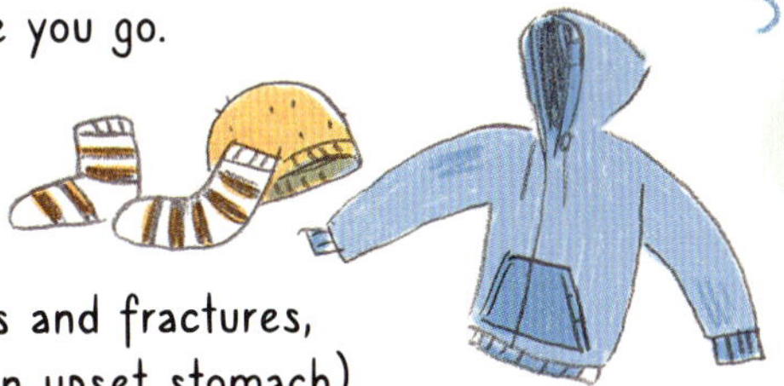

- [ ] Warm clothes and waterproof layers
- [ ] First aid kit (including bandages for sprains, cuts and fractures, antiseptic wipes, painkillers and medication for an upset stomach)

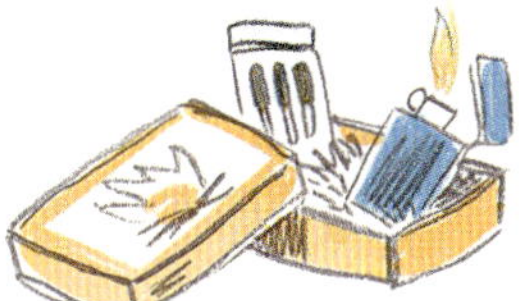

- [ ] Tinder box (including lighter, tinder, waterproof matches)
- [ ] Map and compass

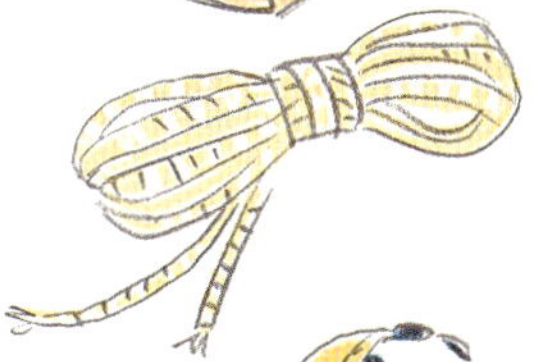

- [ ] Cord (you'll find endless uses for this in the wild)
- [ ] Bug spray (to keep away mosquitoes and midges)

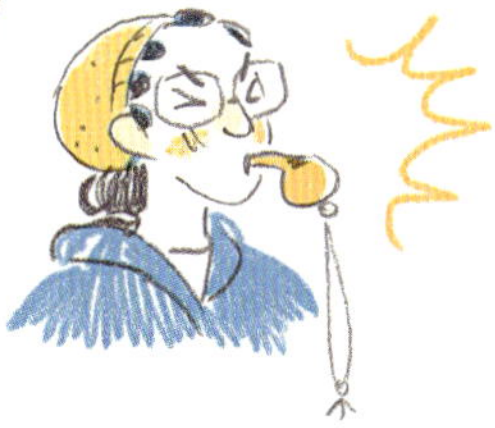

- [ ] A whistle to call for help (hopefully never needed)
- [ ] Water filter and/or water purifying tablets (so you'll never have to use Moyo's moss-sock method)

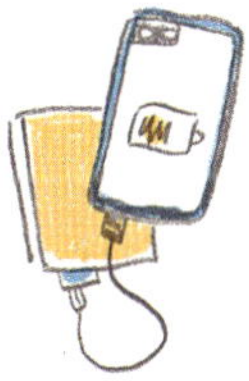

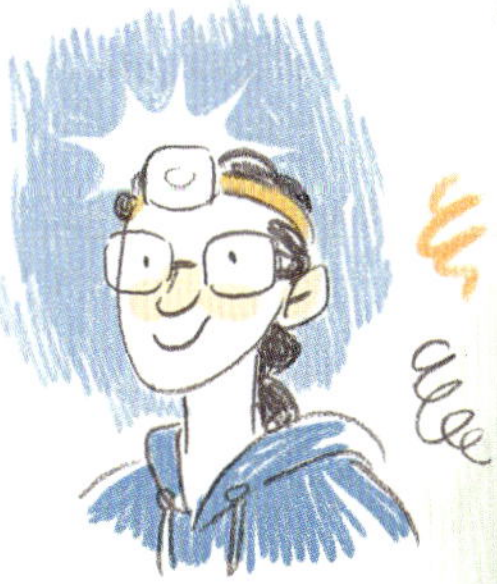

- [ ] Sunscreen
- [ ] Portable phone charger
- [ ] Headlight (plus spare batteries)
- [ ] Dry bag (or at least a spare plastic bag to keep things dry in wet weather)

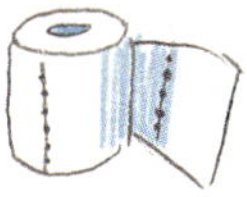

- [ ] Toilet paper (for obvious reasons, plus it's useful as tinder)
- [ ] Emergency flares (mini fireworks that you can set off to signal for help)

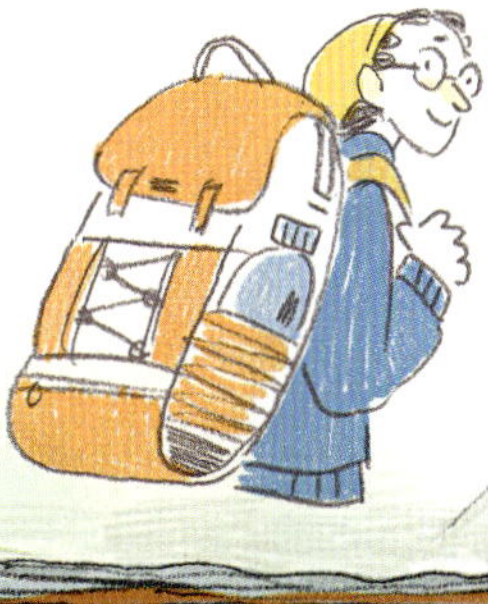

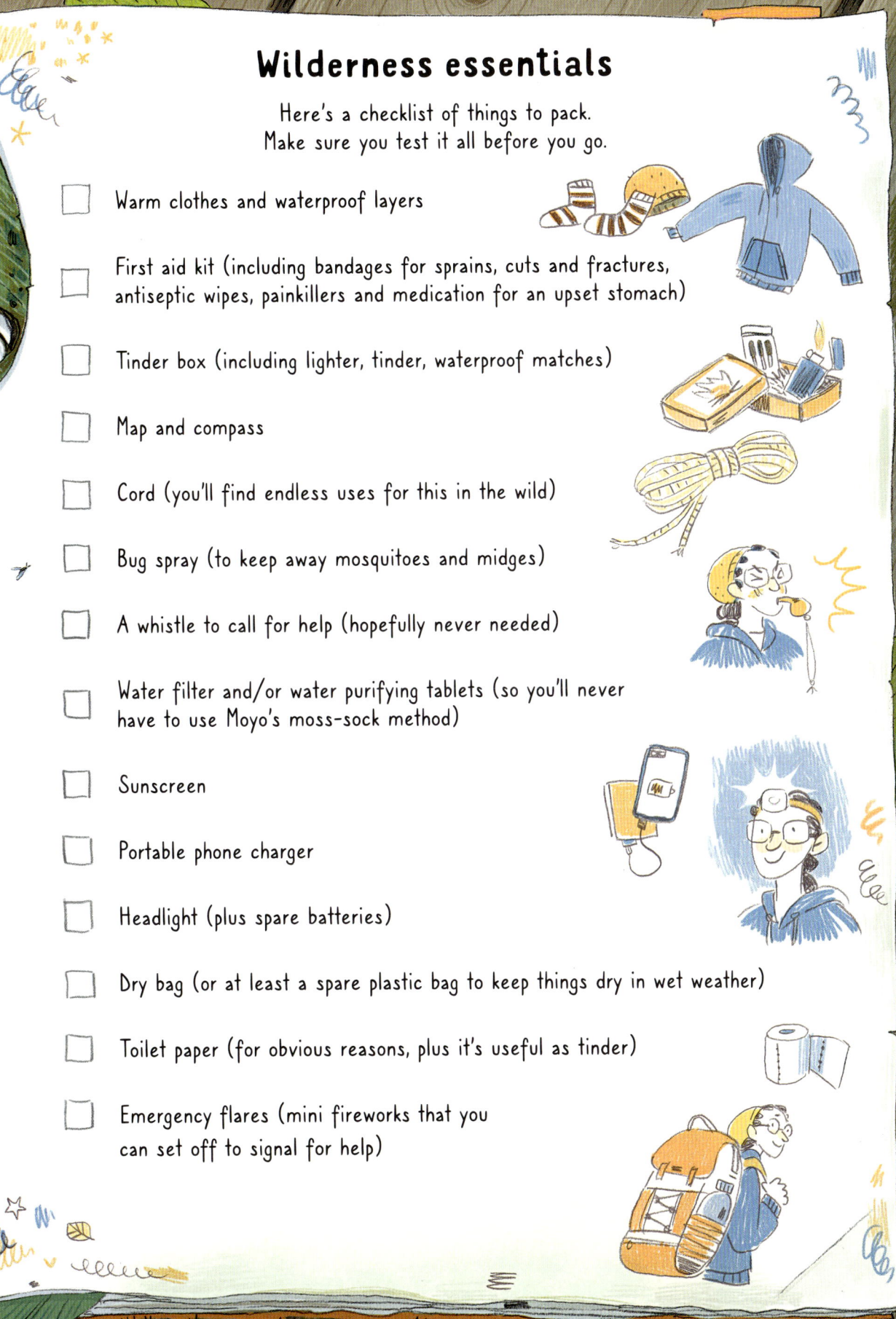

GLOSSARY

This glossary explains some of the words used in this book.
Words written in *italic* type have their own entries.

ACTIVIST – Someone who works to create change in society, often through campaigning and protest.

CONSERVATIONIST – Someone who works to protect wildlife and the environment.

ECOSYSTEM – An area, big or small, where living things interact with one another and their environment.

FIRST NATIONS – *Indigenous peoples* whose ancestors are the first known people to have lived in Canada.

FUNGI – A group of living things, which includes mushrooms, yeasts and toadstools.

GENES – Chemical instructions found in all living things that determine how they're put together, how they behave and what they look like.

HYPOTHERMIA – A dangerous condition that occurs when body temperature drops below 35°C (95°F).

INDIGENOUS PEOPLES – Communities related to the first known people to live in a particular place.

LAND STEWARD – Anyone who respects, protects and cares for the natural world.

PREDATOR – An animal that hunts, kills and eats other animals.

REWILDING – Restoring an area of land to its natural state.

SPECIES – A particular type of animal, plant or other living thing.

SPORES – Tiny things released by *fungi* that allow them to spread and reproduce.

WILDERNESS – A large area of land with most of its original vegetation still intact. These few areas still exist thanks to *land stewards*.

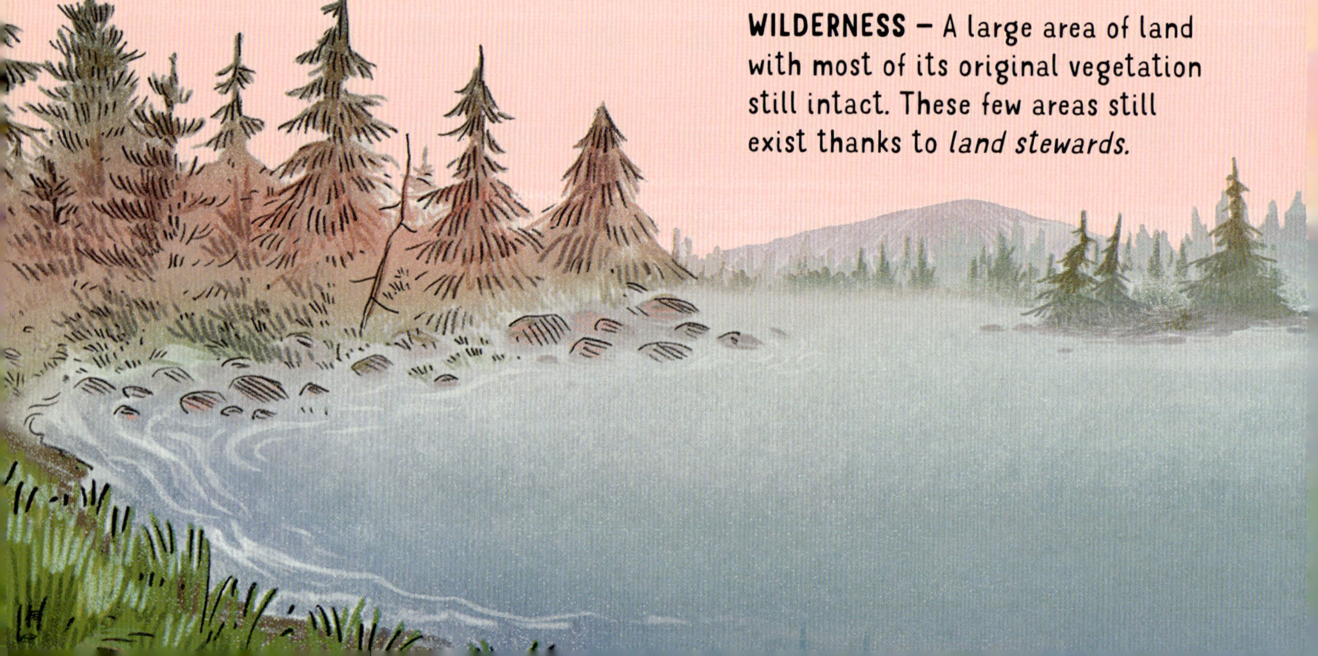

INDEX

The index shows you on which page in the book you'll find things.

B
bats, 4-5, 12-13, 46-47
bears, 14-15, 18-19, 28, 36-37, 38-39, 40-41
  grizzly, 14-15, 41
  spirit, 36-39

C
coastal wolves, 14-15, 24-25
conservation, 8
compass, 12-13, 60-61
cougars, 14-15

D
drinking water, 29, 34, 36, 61

E
eagles, 4, 24

F
firecraft, 5, 6-7, 34
fishing, 22, 35, 37, 44-45, 46-47, 54
foraging, 20-21, 28-29
fungi, 6, 20-21, 28, 47

H
hypothermia, 33

I
Indigenous peoples, 8, 58-59, 60

K
knots, 10

L
life jackets, 51
logging, 8, 22

M
maps, 60-61
moss, 29
Morse code, 55

N
navigation, 12-13, 23

P
porcupines, 27, 47

R
raft building, 48-49, 50-51
rivers, 22-23, 30-31, 32, 35, 42, 52-53

S
salmon, 24, 39, 43, 44-45, 52-53
shelter, 16-17, 33
soil, 27, 46-47

T
tinder, 6-7, 61

Consultants

Rob Ross runs Kaykima Wilderness, teaching survival and bushcraft skills in the Canadian wilderness. He enjoys foraging, wandering the forest and learning new survival skills.

Dr. Regan Early is a senior lecturer in conservation biology at the University of Exeter. She studies the effects of human activity on wildlife around the world.

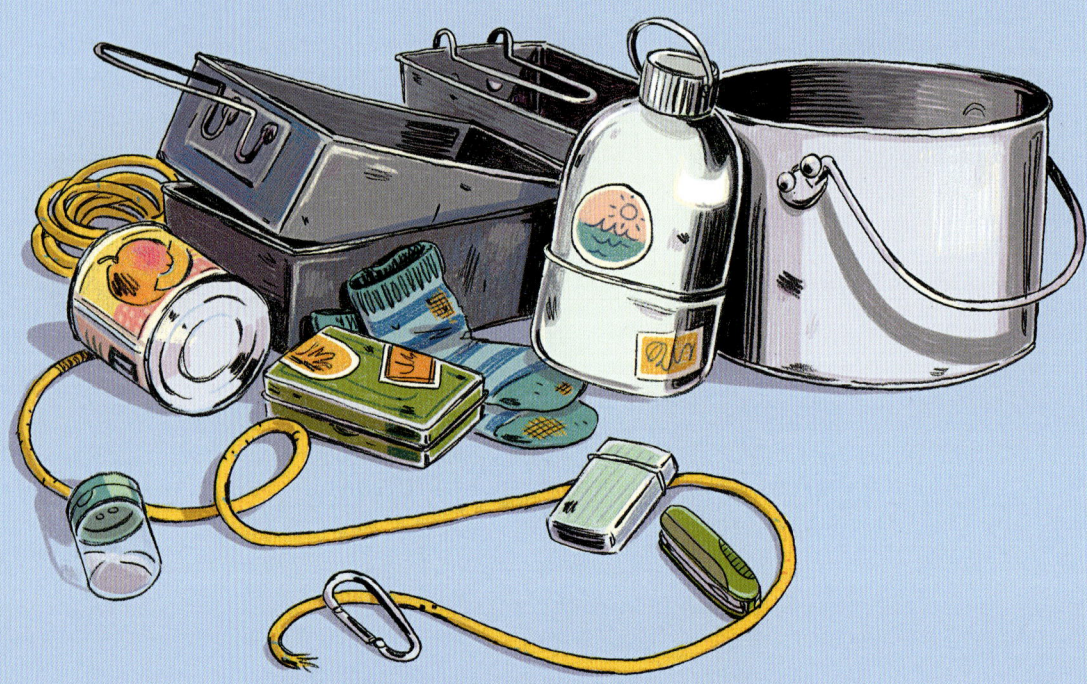

Additional design by Jamie Ball

Digital manipulation by John Russell

Series designer: Laura Wood
Series editor: Ruth Brocklehurst

First published in 2025 by Usborne Publishing Limited,
83-85 Saffron Hill, London EC1N 8RT, United Kingdom. usborne.com

Copyright © 2025 Usborne Publishing Limited. The name Usborne and the Balloon logo are registered trade marks of Usborne Publishing Limited. All rights reserved. No part of this publication may be reproduced or used in any manner for the purpose of training artificial intelligence technologies or systems (including for text or data mining), stored in retrieval systems or transmitted in any form or by any means without prior permission of the publisher. UE.

Usborne Publishing is not responsible and does not accept liability for the availability or content of any website other than its own, or for any exposure to harmful, offensive or inaccurate material which may appear on the Web. Usborne Publishing will have no liability for any damage or loss caused by viruses that may be downloaded as a result of browsing the sites it recommends.

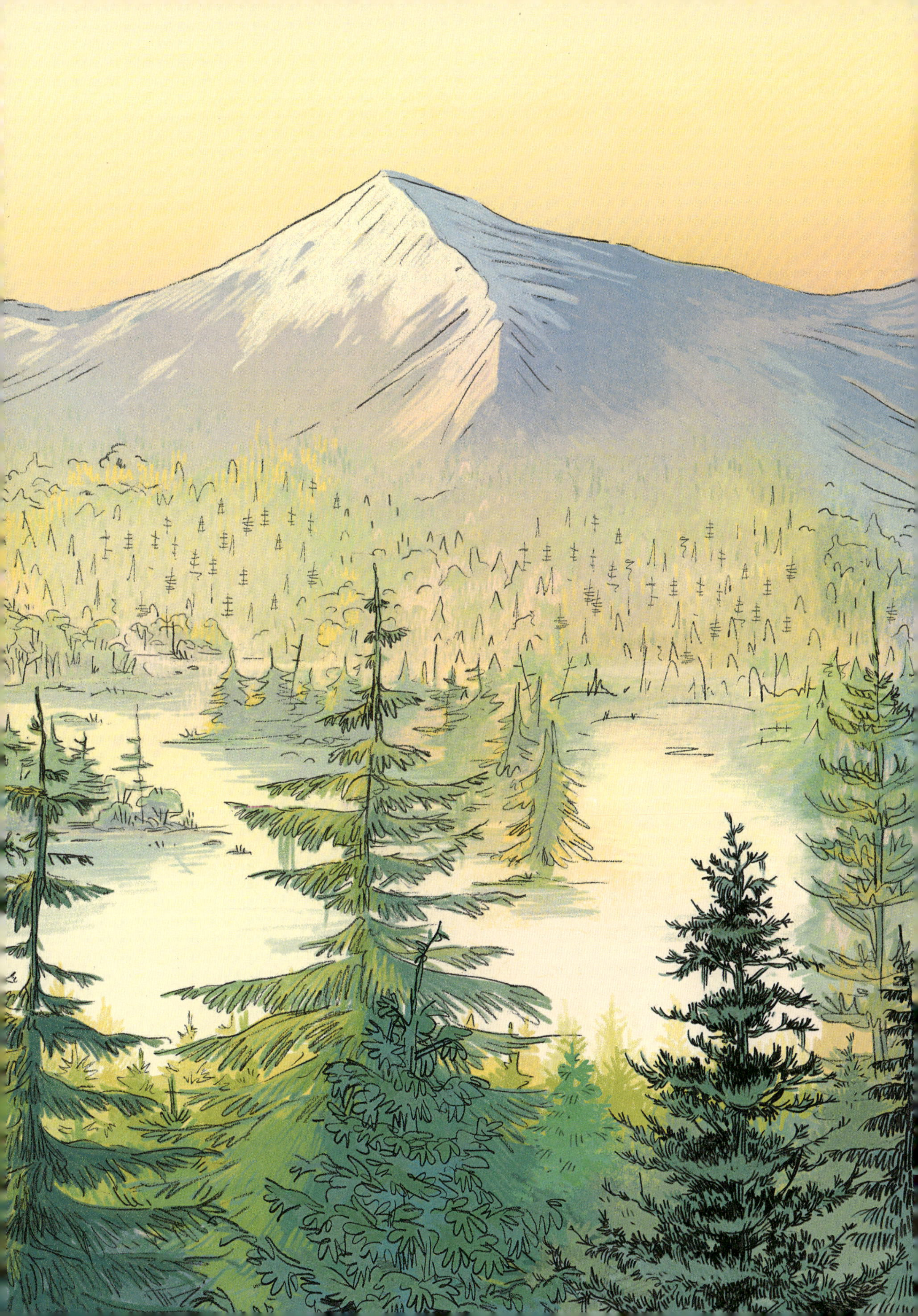

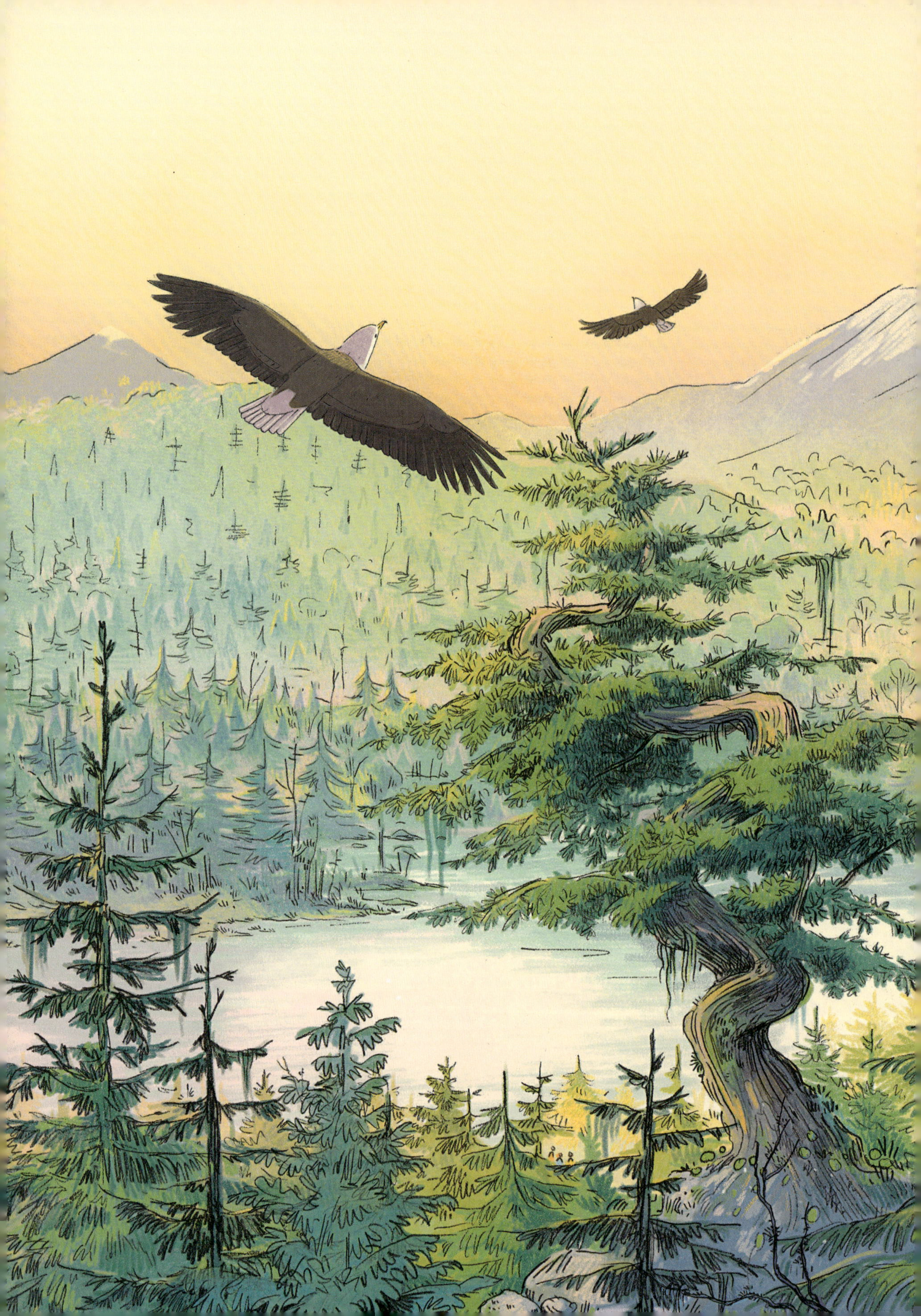